Chronicles of the Infected
Book One

Finding Her

by Rick Wood

Rick Wood

Rick Wood

Dedicated to the memory of George A. Romero – without whom, zombies would have just been an undiscovered dream, rather than an inevitable fate.

Rick Wood

1

The bottom half of his right leg may as well have been ripped off and discarded into a nearby bin. It was a stubborn limb that needn't be there, yet it clung to his knee without purpose or meaning, like a recurring memory that would not fade.

It was an annoyance. It was a burden. But most of all, it was a severe irritation when he was in a hurry. Quite frequently, Gus considered wielding a machete and just chopping the damn thing off.

The leg's ineptness had been an unwelcome present from the Taliban that saw him discharged from the army without so much as a thank you. A bullet from a Kalashnikov assault rifle was lodged deep within the dead tissue of his right calf muscle, and it was a bullet that no doctor had been brave enough to remove. The pain was ongoing, but had grown tolerable; in the way that one could get used to a constant itching that won't go away. The only times he ever really noticed it was either when it hindered his speed, or when puss chose to seep out; which often happened at the most inconvenient of times.

Wasn't exactly a great conversation starter at a dinner party, was it?

"Oh, Gus, just so you know, your leg is leaking

again."

Pathetic.

As he snarled at the dead weight slowing him down, he rushed through the high street toward his motorbike.

Something was happening.

He had no idea what exactly it was, but he knew it wasn't good. His older brother had always been into zombie movies, and Gus had always mocked him, telling him he was watching an unrealistic pile of trash and would be better off watching something that actually made sense.

How little he knew.

He had witnessed enough atrocities within the last hour to fill a whole tour of Afghanistan.

It had started small.

An elderly lady had fallen as she stepped off the bus. As she lay there, her body had convulsed like a dead fish thrashing for life. A crowd then proceeded to gather. One person had announced he was a doctor, and leant in to take her pulse.

Her eyes opened. A sudden jolt. A twisted expression, like she was full of energetic anger, like there was a savage mania rising within her. Cloudy drool trickled across her chin.

She stared at his open throat stretching out before her. Her jaw ripped open, and her sparse remaining teeth clamped into the tasty neck of the doctor.

The gathered crowd immediately dispersed. What had been enquiries of concern rapidly turned into shrieks of terror. Grimaces of sympathy and wishes to help warped into faces of innocents ensuring their own survival.

The doctor had sprung to his feet within seconds.

The professional, caring visage was replaced with a yellow-eyed, carnivorous monster. It was inhuman – that was the only way Gus could describe the creature that rose; *inhuman.*

It sprinted, snarling as it ran.

And boy, could it run.

Gus had never seen a person run so fast. The doctor overtook innocent bystanders fleeing upon bicycles with the ease of a morning stroll. He'd bitten a nearby bike-enthusiast, who had gotten up and bitten a nearby child kicking a ball against the wall, who had gotten up and bitten a policeman trying to intervene.

So many were attacked and ripped apart, yet each and every one of them stood back up. Never mind how much they had been ravaged; never mind what fell out of their open torsos or hung off their mutilated faces – they stood up, and looked to feed.

Those people who had been murdered, brutalised, destroyed, ripped apart – they climbed to their feet and bestowed their fate upon others. Running, bloody drool soaking their chins, ignoring their missing intestines, not caring about their arm that flew away in the aerodynamic resistance of their speed.

All they seemed to want was to feed – and feed they did.

Gus had considered helping. With his military experience, he could have calmed the situation, maybe even prevented chaos. But in the time he had taken to consider this, chaos had already ensued.

How had this happened? Just a moment before Gus was buying milk; now the street had turned into an orgy of violence. It spread so fast he hadn't been able to make sense of it. He lived in a small town on the outskirts of London, with a post office where everyone knew the clerk's name, with a Bargain Booze that recognised the underage teenagers who always tried to buy alcohol, to the local pub whose barman greeted Gus by name – all of it had turned into a decoration of barbarity. Blood splashed across the post office windows, a loose head smashed against the shutters of Bargain Booze, and a horde of infected had filled the pub and devoured everyone within it.

The town centre had turned from a budding working-class community and a peaceful town of cohabitation to a free-for-all open buffet littered with pieces of residents who had known each other by face or name. No one running by foot could react quickly enough – and even that minority who did make a hasty getaway were eventually caught and butchered. A happy toddler nibbling on a lolly screeched as it bit into the throat of its father and bathed in its blood. A young girl passionately kissing her teenage lover abruptly found that kiss turning into a bite, and the skin of her boyfriend's face was stuck in her sharp teeth. Even a baby suckling on its mother's breast growled as its eyes turned and it sank its underdeveloped teeth into its loving parent, forcing her to yelp with tears as her child ripped her mammary gland clean off.

Gus had only one thought on his mind.

My family.

Ignoring the searing pain of the bullet stuck inside his leg, he revved his motorbike into action and twisted through the streets, avoiding as much death and mayhem as he could. It was as if the entire civilisation had turned to madness. Cars beeped manically as they drove into each other, barely able to outrun the racing, rampaging creatures. Gus weaved in and out of wayward vehicles with as much precision and haste as his Marauder would allow him.

Still, their faces circled his thoughts. Those he loved.

My wife. My daughter.

Probably barricaded in their family home.

Once he reached the bypass, the numbers of these monsters grew sparse and he was able to avoid hitting any.

One group of infected attempted to run after him. They almost kept pace they were so fast, but he lurched his motorbike forward and managed to lose them.

With his spare hand, he dialled Janet's number.

"Janet? Janet?"

"Gus! Please! Help us!"

His body tensed. Terror consumed him, hairs on his arm stuck on end, his brow furiously perspiring.

His wife. His childhood sweetheart.

His four-year-old daughter.

Janet.

Laney.

"Janet, are you okay?"

"Have you seen the news? They are saying London has gone to madness. The army quarantined us. They are telling anyone still alive to leave the city we don't have long!"

Shit.

He knew the military's ruthless mindset well enough to know that they meant it. If London was the main hive of this mess, he knew they would simply shut the gates. And, to anyone who was left inside... well, may the Lord take pity upon their souls.

"I'm on my way to you, Janet, is Laney there?"

"Yes, she's here."

"Hide. Take her and hide somewhere in the house, whatever it takes, just–"

"Gus!"

Janet's high-pitched scream pounded harshly against his eardrums, but despite the harsh ache against his ear, Gus did not move the phone away.

"Janet? Janet?!"

She did not respond.

Her screams continued to echo, growing distant.

"*Janet!*"

The call ended.

No...

He would not let them down. He couldn't. They were all he had.

He would die before he let any harm come to them.

He picked up his speed. He twisted the handles, forcing the bike to accelerate, swinging around the corners at such dangerous speed he surprised himself that he managed to keep balance.

His calf stung, but he ignored it. He didn't have the luxury of acknowledging pain.

He passed his local neighbourhood, ignoring the loving family next door getting set upon by a group of undead youths.

He brought his bike to a sudden stop, allowing it to collapse as he jumped off and ran across his porch.

A lump grew in his throat. There were already so many infected visible through the smashed windows of his living room. Groaning. Searching. Clawing at one another to find the family hid within. They descended upon his family home like flies upon shit.

He reached under a garden gnome and took out a knife. Janet had told him he was ridiculous for being so paranoid, that no one from the Taliban was going to come hunting for him, and that he needed help.

For the first time, he was glad she was wrong.

The hallway was crowded with undead. He used his muscle weight to launch himself forward, forcing them aside like a bowling ball into stubborn pins. He snarled and screamed and wretched and growled as he dug his knife into one throat, into the skull of another, into the cheek of another.

He tried to tread his way through, but there were so many, and they were piling on top of him.

He swiped his knife back and forth, back and forth, repeatedly back and forth. He took out whoever he could, slicing throats, dislodging guts, and smearing the blood of their skulls over the loving family pictures he'd hung upon the wall.

As he twisted his knife into another neck, he sent the heavy fist of his free hand into another face and climbed the stairs.

"Janet!"

All he could hear were snarls.

Then he stopped. Stood still. Motionless.

He saw her.

Janet's empty face as she stumbled out of the bedroom.

Except, they were no longer Janet's eyes.

Her face was pale like theirs. Her cheek was missing, revealing a torn skull bone beneath the gap in her flesh. She limped forward, a mocking imitation of his awkward strut. Her pupils were yellow and her eyes were red.

Behind her was a four-year-old girl.

His four-year-old girl.

Crawling across the floor. Both of her legs missing, entrails dragging behind her from her absent waist.

"No…" he gasped.

It couldn't be true.

He had arrived in time. He was sure of it. He must have. He *must* have.

But there they were.

Murdered. Ripped apart. Helpless.

If only he'd have driven faster. Gotten to his motorbike sooner. It could have been seconds, that's all, just seconds.

If only his damn leg hadn't held him back.

Had his daughter's legs been ripped off whilst she was alive?

Was she forced to watch?

Did his wife do it?

Did his daughter have to watch as her own mother–

No. No, she couldn't have.

It couldn't be true…

Just a few seconds earlier… If only…

His wife. His childhood sweetheart. The woman he had loved since he was sixteen. The woman he had proposed to atop the hill where he had first confessed his love for her.

His daughter. Conceived after years of trying.

Their loving creation.

Both clambering toward him with nothing but evil in their eyes, desperate to kill him, desperate to tear him apart.

No.

No, it can't be.

This is a fate worse than death.

Just a few seconds, that's all it would have taken. Just a few seconds more.

He did the best thing he could for them.

Wiping tears away on his sleeve, he slid his knife into the skull of his wife.

He crouched beside his daughter. His loving, doting daughter, who had just learnt to read. Who had just learnt to add.

Don't do this... he thought. *Don't do this...*

He ignored his own protestations.

He drove the knife into the back of his daughter's skull.

The rest of them burst through the door, their open hands grabbing for him.

And even though he jumped out of the window, he left himself in that house with his family. His wife. His daughter. And the walls he had built around them.

And although he survived, he didn't. That day, he became the person who lived in a home with no mirrors because he couldn't bear to look in one. That day, he decided forevermore to see everyone, and everything, as the enemy.

That day, Gus Harvey both lived, and died.

Rick Wood

Six months later

Rick Wood

2

London was tearing itself apart.

Not metaphorically, not symbolically, and not in any way one may interpret a tired cliché – London *was* tearing itself apart, in the complete, literal meaning of the word. It was utter anarchy.

For the undead it was a place of safety, where you would be squashed among many, fighting for the rare pieces of meat left in the quarantined zone like a pack of feral pigeons competing for torn pieces of bread; except that slice of bread was the flesh of the poor, helpless human who had managed to survive the city's chaos long enough to simply die in that moment.

Upon the onset of the zombie apocalypse the government had been quick to act, despite Parliament's depleting numbers. Even though the highest-ranked members of Parliament had been eaten or transformed into the infected within days, they had still created well-kept and well-hidden plans for what to do in the event of a viral outbreak. Although the cause of the chaos was unknown, these plans were deemed competent enough to be put into action immediately.

Part of this plan involved separating the central part of the outbreak from the rest of the country. In this case, that meant the capital city.

London was the hive of the undead. Yes, the population of walking corpses existed across the country, but in more dense numbers; numbers the authorities had deemed more manageable. London, however, was home to the vast numbers of jaw-snapping, flesh-seeking, maggot-ridden, living undead. Within days, almost the entire living population of the city had been wiped out and replaced by hungry beasts with one instinct – to feed.

There was only one solution:

Get rid of London.

Wooden walls were mounted and, although they shivered against the weight of the hundreds of thousands of bodies pushing against them, they stood sturdily enough to contain what could be contained.

Outside of London had seen its own rising, but with more sparse populations, the death toll hadn't been the same. You would likely cross a gang of them on the road whilst out driving, or even get chased down by one on the way home. People still died every day – but through being surprised by the few, not descended upon by the thousands.

General Boris Hayes stood atop the wall, gazing pitifully upon the wretched faces that used to have a soul, and now did nothing but hunt and feed.

He assumed they had caught his faint scent from afar and surged toward him, as they were now amassing in devastating quantities. They reached up, helplessly scraping for the face peering down at them, driven by nothing but their animalistic urges. Their bodies moved with a disjointed peculiarity, yet they travelled with the speed of exceptional sprinters. They pounded against the wall that quivered beneath Hayes, yet their clambering hands did nothing to break or falter his hateful gaze.

He would never be deterred by the enemy. Saddam Hussain never scared him. The Taliban never scared him. He could have come face-to-face with Bin Goddamn Laden and the entirety of Al Qaeda and he still would have laughed mockingly as he spat in their faces. He would die before he allowed the enemy to dent his pride.

But this was something else.

These undead creatures were not driven by a lust for power or a hatred of the West; they were driven by something far stronger. They were quick, robust, and determined to get their prey. They could smell him, sense him, perhaps even hear the blood pumping through his veins. Given the opportunity, they would sink their teeth in him, rip the skin from his bones, and feast upon his bloody entrails.

On their own they were a formidable opponent. But as an army...

It was staggering.

Hayes peered into the city, down the streets, and he could not see the end of them. The city was bursting, full of them, hundreds of thousands snarling below him, craving his living flesh.

The only thing Hayes could say against them is that they weren't organised. But, with such numbers and such strength, they didn't need to be.

His radio hissed a crackle of static and a voice sounded through the speaker.

"Hayes, are you receiving, over?"

Hayes picked the radio off his belt and lifted it to

his mouth. Only his arm moved. The rest of his body remained in his military at-ease stance, his feet shoulder-width apart, his left hand behind his back.

"This is Hayes."

"General, we have eyes, we are ready to deploy, over."

"What's the ETA?"

"To get the bombs all coordinated over target and ready, we estimate detonation in T-minus two days six hours, over."

Two days.

That's how long it took them to arrange a bunch of explosives.

"Two days?"

"It's the best we could do, over."

"Where's our fire-power?"

"In the rubble of Great Britain, sir. Over."

He sighed.

Two days six hours until this city would be destroyed. For two more days, these ravenous arseholes would continue to batter against the walls. Without these bombs, Hayes knew they would need to reinforce the walls further, and even then, they probably wouldn't hold. With the numbers and the strength and the sheer speed they could run at it with, it was only a matter of time. And if this horde was let loose, if they were to escape – that would be the country gone. They outnumbered the remaining military, not to mention the sad truth Hayes had to admit – their power would overwhelm any defence they were to put up on the ground.

It was true. They had no choice but to wait for the reinforcements to arrive. They were lucky that they had enough allies to spare the firepower in a time of crisis.

"Roger," Hayes reluctantly confirmed. "ETA fifty-four hours."

"Confirmed, over."

"Over and out."

He placed the radio back on his belt.

He cast his glare over the creatures.

The noise was overwhelming; continuous growls, snarls, drooling. But that wasn't what hit him the most.

It was the smell.

They smelt like death.

Hayes had been around enough of it to recognise the stench. It was distinctive. Like rotting meat.

Once upon a time, the smell had made him choke. Made him feel sick, even made him a little dizzy.

Now it had as much effect on him as someone leaving a foul turd in his toilet bowl.

It was a mild nuisance, but something he had come to tolerate.

But these zombies...

These foul creatures...

These disgusting, carnivorous, detestable hordes of the ravenous undead.

Hayes would not tolerate them.

London was going up in flames.

Each rotting face would be burnt until they were incinerated.

"I'll be seeing you later," Hayes muttered at the despicable pale, rotting, flesh-torn faces below him.

He climbed back down and returned to his vehicle, setting aim for the acting prime minister.

3

Eugene Squire stood solemnly at his window, overlooking the vast, empty streets below.

Empty of people, anyway. Nights generally left the town deserted of anyone living. But the infected never slept. They were relentless.

He watched as another infected hobbled past, dragging its leg behind it, its ankle missing its foot. Its greying face had a prickly moustache home to various pieces of mould, and an eye that hung down its cheek by a loose string of flesh.

This isn't what they were meant for...

A brusque commotion announced itself down the street. A young girl came screaming down the road. She couldn't be older than thirteen. She was followed by a gang of flesh-eating parasites at a far quicker pace, closing the gap on her quickly. Eugene briefly wondered if there was something he could do to save the girl, but that wasn't the world he lived in anymore. Trying to be a hero would likely cost him his life. She was on her own.

He closed his curtains.

His thoughts dwelled on the girl. Then he realised it didn't matter.

He turned around and sighed, absentmindedly

shuffling through a stack of papers on his grand wooden desk. He had always resented how the other half live, despite being part of that other half. He was used to just sitting in a Parliament building either heckling agreement or disagreement at whatever fool was speaking.

Now the government was gone. Hundreds had died. And he just so happened to be the next in line to be acting prime minister.

He had appeared to accept the job reluctantly. He had to have been. It was the only way he would be endowed the power to see this through.

A knock resounded against his doors.

"Come in."

Jacey entered, a young man who had led many expeditions into the wild, hunting animals and missing souls. Eugene had been sure his youth and experience made him the perfect person for the job, and he had been paid handsomely in response.

Jacey indicated to the rest of his team to remain outside, and edged in nervously.

"Any news?" Eugene asked.

Before Jacey could respond, General Boris Hayes knocked on the door and entered.

"Boris, is it urgent?" Eugene enquired.

"It is," Hayes assured him.

"Fine, fine, wait there." Eugene waved his arm flippantly, indicating the corner of the room, and turned back to Jacey. "So?"

"We've tracked her, sir," Jacey told him with a worryingly grim expression.

"Really?" Eugene moved from foot to foot, barely able to keep still, wandering aimlessly around. "And?

Where is she?"

"That's the thing, sir. We tracked her location, but... We couldn't go in."

"Why?"

"We have absolute certainty she is there, it's just–"

"Bloody hell, Jacey, for Christ's sake, where is she?"

"She's in–" Jacey's eyes nervously averted themselves from Eugene's. "She's in a building in London."

A lost look painted itself upon his face. A look that appeared to be someone who'd been hopeful, then had that hope snatched away and burnt before him.

Everyone knew London was a no-go. It was a quarantined zone, with so many wretched infected, that not even the most adeptly trained and highly skilled fighter would be able to make it inches across the wall.

He turned to Hayes.

"You have to get her."

"That's not as simple as you'd expect," Hayes responded. "I came here with news. We have bombs on their way from multiple sources. London will be dust in T-minus two days, four hours."

Eugene appeared stumped.

"My God..." he muttered. He brought a stutter to his lips, showing a lack of ability to speak, to move. "Call it off!"

"Negative. It's all been put in place. They are being readied as they are; it can't be reversed. Sir, if we go back on it now, our allies may not be so amiable next time. London *will* be bombed."

Eugene's feet gave way, and he used the desk to steady himself.

"Why the hell not?"

"Prime Minister, the bombs are coming from multiple sources. We could not manage to get the message to all of them in time; and even if we managed to call off a few, we could not be sure to reach all of them. Not in the state the world is currently in."

"Well then, deploy the army! Send them in there to retrieve her!"

Hayes sighed.

"Negative."

"What the hell do you mean, negative?" Eugene shouted, a face full of rage, scalding anger spewing out of his mouth. "I am the fucking prime minister! If I tell the army to go in, they go in!"

Hayes hesitated. "No one would be willing to go into London. No one. And even if they could – we are at your service for all country needs, but this is personal. I'm sorry."

"You're sorry?" Eugene venomously spat. He had to keep this up. He had to seem hysterical. "You can stuff your sorry up your sorry arse!"

"I *am* sorry," Hayes lied. "The only way is to get someone to volunteer, and I can't see any of my troops volunteering to risk it all for one person."

"That one person is *my god damn daughter!*"

Eugene could feel his blood pumping, feel his fists clenching, feel himself lurching forward. Jacey had already snuck out unnoticed, such was the direction of his rage toward his military leader.

"We have to think about the bigger picture."

An uncomfortable silence overcame the room. Eugene covered his face in his hands, trying to control his fake tears, his fake uncontrollable weeping forcing its way to the surface.

Hayes stood at ease, watching their leader, the unelected man in charge by default.

Then an idea grew.

An idea Hayes was certain he would regret voicing.

"There is one person," Hayes slowly articulated. "One person we could ask. One person I think we could persuade."

"Who?" Eugene said. "Tell me, who? And I'll give them whatever they want."

Hayes sighed a sigh of hesitation.

"Gus Harvey."

Eugene froze.

"Gus Harvey?" he repeated.

Hayes reluctantly nodded.

"Are you fucking kidding me?" Eugene couldn't believe what he was hearing.

"He is our last resort, but I think he'll do it."

"But – but – but he's a drunk!"

"Yes, but the guy basically wants to die. He's the only one crazy enough, or doesn't care enough, to do it."

Eugene scoffed. He stood and found himself drifting toward the window.

"We could send that Donny boy with him, sir," Hayes suggested. "I think we could convince him to be in charge of communications for the mission. He doesn't have much else going on for him, he could at least report back on progress."

Eugene hovered, looking upon the dark street below. The remains of the young girl were left strewn across the ground. Her lungs, her heart, her legs, her limbs, her eyeball. All left squished in bloody heaps where she had been fed upon and left. Her head still remained, barely recognisable, but groaning in its catatonic zombie state.

He wondered whether she knew her body had been ripped away, or whether she even had the awareness to know what a body was.

"Well?" Hayes prompted.

Eugene took a big, deep breath, held it, and released.

Gus Harvey was inept. An uncontrollable wreck. A drunk. He didn't stand a chance. He'd off himself at the first opportunity. And Donny was an imbecile. The lad would screw up a boiled egg, he was such an idiot.

It was a disaster in the making.

Perfect.

"Send for him. Get him here immediately."

"Roger that," Hayes responded, and hastily left the room.

4

A trickle of spilt whiskey dribbled down the bedsheets, exploding in a small pool upon the stained carpet. A busy fly fluttered over Gus's closed eyes, prompting an automatic slap of his own face that abruptly woke him from his vegetative state.

"Fuck!" he growled, hazily flickering his eyelids as he rotated his head, readjusting his drunken vision to the blurs of the room.

A whiskey bottle lay upside down on his duvet, leaking the entirety of its contents; which Gus considered to be an act of sacrilege.

"Aw, shit!" he huffed, punching his heavy fist into the bottle, immediately regretting it as his palm delved into a few shards of glass.

He held his bleeding wrist in his hand, at first pressing against the wound, then deciding he couldn't be bothered to hold the position and ignored it. He pushed himself off the bed, leaving a bloody handprint in his wake.

He trudged his hefty weight – a weight that was once from muscle, but had turned to excessive fatty width and extra insulation – and limped across his bedsit. He lifted his wounded leg and placed it in the sparse areas of the floor vacant from litter, dirty clothes, or mouldy plates. His limp had been as engrained into his demeanour as much as his voice or his thoughts, and he had even grown a resentful fondness for the bullet lodged in his calf.

His chubby hand clutched the fridge door, opened it, and withdrew a supermarket own-brand can of lager. He poured it down his gullet like a child feeding on his mother's tit.

He meandered to the window, peering at the street below, checking that the world had still gone to shit.

He scorned the rising of another shitty day, angry that he had not somehow died in his sleep. It took him so many drinks and so many pills to fall into his catatonic state, he always hoped that it would be enough booze and meds to leave him in it.

He sighed.

There was nothing to do.

No itinerary other than to mope around his shitty little flat, miserable at his pointless existence, draining the world's depleting resources that could otherwise help someone who actually wanted to be in this damn life.

There were no cinemas. No schools. And worst of all, no bars. No classic British pub he could go sit in and get wasted at the bar, lamenting his drunken troubles to whatever unfortunate barmaid was made to work that day.

The schools had been turned into extra hospitals.

The pubs had been turned into places of refuge.

Eugene Squire had managed to put some semblance of society into this forsaken world in his unwarranted few months in charge, but they were a long way off being close to the life they had. In all honesty, they would likely never be able to have it back again.

Gus would never be able to have them back again.

A boom punched against his door.

A visitor?

"What the hell…" he mumbled.

No one visited him. He had barely spoken to another human being since…

Since it happened.

The boom repeated itself, growing impatient.

"Who is it?" he barked.

"Open the bloody door, man!" came a voice Gus recognised.

He waddled to the door, his right leg stiff. This was possibly the quickest he'd had to move with a wounded leg since…

Stop thinking about it. Just stop thinking about any of it.

He swung the door open and lifted his nose in revulsion at the sight of General Boris Hayes.

"What are you doing here?" Gus demanded with a low-pitched hostility.

"Your country needs you, Gus."

"Go to hell."

Gus returned to his messy bedsit and resumed gulping the remains of his can of lager.

He could feel Hayes looking around his home, sticking his nose up at how Gus chose to live.

To hell with him. This was Gus's accommodation, and he liked – well, tolerated it.

"This is where you live now, is it?" Hayes asked, a clear dig aimed at how Gus's life had gone from military hero to pathetic loser in such a shattering fall.

"What's it got to do with you?"

"You know, we have grand flats and lovely houses that have been vacated, all without owners."

"You want me to steal some dead man's home?"

"They won't be needing it."

Gus snorted a sarcastic laugh. "That's all the dead are to you, ain't they? To be discarded."

"Yes, well, I preferred the dead when they didn't try to get up and eat me."

"Weren't those the days," Gus retorted mockingly, crumpling the empty can and throwing it in the mess on the floor. He looked out the window, keeping his back to his former leader. "You want to tell me what you came here for, or what? I doubt you came for a social call."

Hayes hesitated.

"No, I didn't. Like I said, your country is requesting your service. There is a mission for you to undertake. And, still being under the paycheck of the military, you are unable to decline."

Gus snorted.

"That how you persuade me, is it? Threaten to take money away?"

"I was going to appeal to your better nature, but I assumed it would fall on deaf ears."

"And this mission you say I'm requested for. I imagine the only reason you came to me is because no other fool is willing to take it. Probably a suicidal mission, I bet."

"You would be accurate. So, are you coming or what? I don't have all day."

Gus turned to look at Hayes, folding his arms and leaning against the window-sill.

"You wouldn't come to a cripple has-been like me

unless you had no choice."

"Like I said, are you coming or not?"

"Not. You can go to hell. And you can shut my bloody door on the way out."

Hayes closed his eyes in angry frustration, flexing his hands in an act intended to calm himself down. Gus could see the fury flickering on Hayes's face as he tried to resist losing his temper, and did not feel guilty in deriving a small amount of pleasure in seeing him squirm.

"Eugene Squire, our acting prime minister, is the one requesting your presence, Gus."

"Like I said, you can fuck off. I ain't going nowhere."

"For God's sake, do you not care about anyone but yourself anymore?"

Gus let out a loud, clearly audible, "Hah!"

Hayes shook his head in irritation.

"I'll take that as a no," Hayes mused.

"You can take that as a fuck off. Once again."

Hayes's eyes meandered around Gus's flat, eventually falling on a photo frame hidden behind a pile of dirty clothes. It was of Gus, in his military uniform, next to a doting wife and a loving daughter.

"They would hate to see you like this, you know."

Gus immediately marched forward, ignoring the searing pain in his leg. Once he reached the general, he put his hands on his collar and shoved him against the door frame.

"You don't say a bloody word about them, do you hear?"

"I was attempting to appeal to your better nature."

Assuming a tight grip upon Hayes's collar, he

pulled him out of the flat, shoved him into the corridor, and slammed the door behind him.

He paused, feeling the rage shoot through his veins, feeling his hostility consume him.

He looked at the photo.

He peered into her eyes.

Peered into both of their eyes.

How pathetic he had become.

He bowed his head.

Sighed.

"Idiot," he muttered to himself.

Gus grabbed his coat and swung the door open.

"This better be bloody worth it," he croaked, and followed Hayes to his car.

5

Gus peered around the lavish corridor leading to Eugene Squire's office with a mixture of awe and resentment.

Statues surrounded his path through the corridor, pieces of history decorating the walls. White beams ran up the wall and over the ceiling, sculpted into impressive pieces of architecture that twisted and turned into various positions. Expensive paintings hung over perfectly applied wallpaper, the eyes of historical monarchs following him as he passed through.

Even the smell of the corridor was distinct. It smelt clean and scented, unlike the burning and rotting flesh that consumed the air outside.

It was wrong.

Wrong that someone should live in such luxury when the rest of the world fought for survival. Roaming through these corridors allowed one to be completely unaware of the horrors at their doorstep.

Even the rich don't get perturbed in the apocalypse...

He followed Hayes to a door with wooden indents and a gold-coloured door handle. After knocking gently, Hayes awaited confirmation and walked in, followed by Gus.

Gus set his eyes on Eugene with pre-judgement. The way he stood was that of a privately educated man, and the way he looked upon Gus was like that of a man who knew little about true suffering. Yet, his eyes were moist, and his face was a disgruntled frown. Something had upset him.

"Gus Harvey," Eugene acknowledged, sticking out his hand. "It's a pleasure."

Gus looked upon the hand like Eugene was offering him shit on a stick.

"You wash those hands with fancy hand wash?" Gus asked.

"I beg your pardon?" Eugene retracted his hand and looked back at Gus with confusion.

"I asked whether you wash those hands with fancy hand wash," Gus retorted, pronouncing each and every syllable with full articulation.

Eugene shot Hayes a look, as if the general could offer an explanation. Hayes returned the look with a shrug.

"You'll have to excuse me, but I don't quite understand what you're asking."

"I was just thinking, as I walked through your lovely building, whether you have cleaners that make it smell like blossoming flowers," Gus said. "Whether you have someone who will wipe your arse and bring you your expensive hand wash."

Gus stepped closer to Eugene so he was placing the politician entirely in his shadow.

"Most of all, I was wondering whether you have a nice, big, secure lock on your door? 'Cause it would be a shame for some nasty undead people to knock it down and ruin that perfect smell."

Gus's eyes remained focussed on Eugene's, and he took a moment of rare pleasure in seeing Eugene looking intimidated, like a child in trouble.

Eugene backed away and edged to the security of behind his desk, where he continued to gaze worriedly at Gus.

"I assume this is a dig at me living in a nice, big house after the world has gone to the dogs?"

"Somethin' along those lines…"

"Well, I would ask you – if you had the choice to do your work in a nice house or a not so nice house, which one would you choose?"

"You say that, but you ain't seen my bedsit." Gus chuckled to himself, looking around the office. Photos of Eugene and his family decorated the furniture. Well-crafted drawers and cupboards adorned the room with a delicate flourish. It was far posher than Gus would ever be comfortable with.

"So," Gus blurted out. "What the fuck am I doing 'ere?"

Eugene blinked his way out of his discomfort at the use of an obscenity.

"Yes, well, I do impress upon you that time is of the essence. We have a mission for you. We need you to go to London to recall a target."

"A target?"

"Yes. My daughter. She is trapped there."

Gus raised his eyebrows and let out a snigger that enraged Eugene.

"Well, the rich get rich, but they do still suffer the trials of us poor folk. Ain't that a strange kinda justice?"

"Excuse me, but that is my daughter." Eugene spoke with an intense irritation, but it sounded like a mouse helplessly squeaking.

"There's more," offered Hayes. "A few hours ago, we gave the go-ahead for bombs to be dropped on the quarantine zone of London. We have two days."

"Hah!" Gus blurted out, then began talking slowly, taking it all in. "So, you are telling me, that you want me to go into the most dangerous place in the country, racked full of zombies – basically because no one else will do it, I'm willing to wager – and you want me to get your girl out of there, within two days."

"Probably less, now," Eugene replied, his lip stuttering, trying to keep it together. "But yes, that would be fairly accurate."

Gus looked to Hayes. To Eugene. To Hayes. To Eugene.

"As I told your man previously – you can go to hell."

Gus turned and marched toward the door. He grabbed hold of the handle, swung it open, then was made to freeze by a sentence he was not expecting to hear.

"Her name is Laney, Gus."

He remained motionless, his back to the room. His head slowly twisted around, until it was peering over his shoulder at the desperate eyes of the acting prime minister.

"You what?" he grunted, slowly and menacingly.

"That's right, her name is Laney," Eugene confirmed. "Just like your daughter was called."

Gus's blood boiled. His heart raced. A booming headache began pounding against the inside of his skull.

How dare they use his family.

How dare they con him into this like that.

"Let's get this straight," Gus spoke quickly and angrily, turning and jabbing his pointing finger to emphasise his words. "This is going to be done my way."

"Okay," Eugene replied.

"You give me whatever weapons I want."

"Okay."

"You stay the fuck out of my way and you do not oppose any of my methods."

"Okay."

"And if I should die, you don't paint me up as some military hero. You tell the world what a sack of shit I was. I'm not in this for the lies."

"If that's how you want it."

"Right."

Gus turned to go.

"There is one more thing," Eugene said.

"What?"

"I need you to take my media liaison officer to refer back to me and update me on progress."

"I ain't taken no one who's going to slow me down."

"Please, I insist. You can manage the hunt, he can manage communication with me. It means you can concentrate on–"

"Fine, fine!" Gus waved his hand dismissively. "But he better not weigh me down. I'm going into London – fucking *London* – and I ain't prepared to be carrying around a sack of shit that's gonna get me eaten."

"I understand."

"I die on my own terms, you 'ear?"

"I hear you."

"Good." He glanced at Hayes, then back at Eugene. "I leave in twenty minutes."

He stormed out of the office, his war face already on.

6

Donny Jevon screamed as a hundred zombies swarmed toward him.

He bashed the buttons, pressing whichever combinations he knew would get his character to perform an acrobatic sequence of movements that would somehow make his avatar fly-kick his opponents.

But it was no good. He was eaten, screaming to death.

"Balls!" he exclaimed, removing his headset and throwing it at the computer screen. He always failed at the level of this game, and it was getting irritating.

A succession of knocks announced themselves against the door to his office.

(Donny refers to it as his 'office' – though it was more apt to call it a 'basement with a desk.')

He froze. Who on earth would be after him? No one was ever after him.

He was a media liaison officer during the zombie apocalypse – there were hardly many press conferences for him to manage in the country's current situation. The phone wasn't ringing off the hook with lots of people requesting confirmation that yes, they were still screwed, and no, the prime minister did not have a clue what to do about it.

"Donny?" came the voice of Eugene Squire.

"Bollocks!" he squealed in a frantically alarmed high-pitched voice.

He quickly hit ctrl+alt+del on his keyboard, crashing out of the game. He swept his porn magazines off the table and into the bin, shoving the bin back into the corner of the room. Then, in a final attempt to retain some dignity, he speedily stacked all the crumb-covered plates scattered around his office.

"Coming!" he hastily shouted, brushing crisps off his lap and opening the curtains of the tiny, high-up window. He squinted as the high sun entered his dingy workplace and leapt toward the door.

"Hurry up, Donny!" came the impatient voice of his boss, and leader of his country.

"Coming!"

He shifted nervously from foot to foot, anxiously scanning the room for any remaining evidence of procrastination or inappropriate work behaviour. Once he was relatively sure, he opened the door.

"Hi!" he squeaked, his voice breaking at the exact moment he addressed the prime minister.

Eugene burst in, knocking Donny out the way, then abruptly stopped and held his nose.

"Dear God, Donny," he cried. "What on earth is that ghastly smell?"

"Er…" Donny stuttered.

The sound of his computer suddenly blared through his speakers, the noise of his computer game depicting the sorry end of his avatar by the hands of ravenous zombies. The screen came back to life, revealing a pixelated image that distastefully mirrored the real-life horrors occurring outside.

"Really?" Eugene asked, pulling a disgusted expression. "Is that not a bit nasty? Considering all that's going on?"

"It was, er…" Donny's brain spun a hundred miles per hour. "It was research."

Eugene's eyes floated across the room and settled on a pair of breasts staring back at him from a page dumped in the bin.

"And I suppose that is research too?"

"Er…"

Eugene raised his eyebrows expectantly.

"It gets really lonely down here, sir."

"Right." Eugene shook his flustered head. "It feels rather bizarre saying this to you, but I need your help. That is, if you can take yourself away from your computer games and your pornographic material for a few moments."

"Oh, okay, yes." Donny shifted nervously. It had been a while since he had actually been required. "What for? Need me to release a statement? Prepare a speech?"

"No. I need you to go to London."

"What, you mean there's a press conference outside the walls?"

"No, there is no damn press conference. I don't need you to write anything. I need your ability to work the technology. My daughter is stuck inside of London, and it's going to be bombed in approximately two days."

"O… kay…" Donny fiddled with his lip. "And you want me to go into London… to get her?"

"Yes."

"I, er… I don't know what to… That's suicide."

"If you were to go alone, then yes, I imagine you would die in a heartbeat. But you are not."

Donny stuttered, unable to figure out whether that was meant to be reassurance. But before he could protest, Eugene continued.

"Gus Harvey, ex-military, has been tasked with the mission of going into London and retracting her within the allotted time."

"But what good am I?" Donny inquired.

"You are the only person I have left on my staff competent with media equipment. I need you to be my liaison. I need you to update me on Gus's progress. I need to know my daughter is going to be safe."

"But… I wouldn't survive in London…"

"I daren't disagree." Eugene looked over Donny as the incompetent fool Donny felt like. "Very well. You accompany him to London and you wait outside the quarantined zone. You can let me know when he's in, and when he's out."

"I…"

"Get yourself ready, Donny. You leave in ten minutes."

Eugene turned and charged out of his room.

Donny looked back at the office. What he'd give to shut those curtains and get back to his game.

He had a feeling reality would be different.

Rick Wood

Minus Two Days

Rick Wood

7

Gus found it strange to be behind the wheel of a powerful automobile. For so long, he had been used to driving a people carrier, forced to listen to children's nursery rhymes for most of his journeys. Though it always made him smile as his girl sang playfully along in the back...

He shook his head.

Shake it off. They're gone.

He revved the engine, providing a loud distraction. The Ferrari responded with a tumultuous roar, the whirs of the engine growling back at him. He shifted the car into gear, readying the accelerator, craving the smell of burning tyres against the road surface.

The passenger door opened and a young, scrawny man took the seat next to him. He looked boyish, with thin and gangly limbs, a greasy mop atop his head, and ill-fitting clothes hanging off his bony arms.

Gus sneered at the sight of a tattoo across the inside of his forearm that read 'DONNY' in Courier New. Why the hell did this guy have a tattoo of his own god-damn name? In case he forgot it?

What a knobhead.

"Hi, I'm Donny!" he sang out with a cheerfulness that made Gus shiver. As soon as he clipped his seatbelt in, Donny turned his huge, beaming smile toward Gus and held out an eager hand.

Gus glared at the hand.

After a few awkward moments, Donny retracted it.

"So, this is great, huh? An adventure! I'm well excited to get on the road and see some zombie action!"

Was this guy on acid or something? Was he happy the world had gone to hell? What was wrong with him?

"Fruit pastel?" Donny offered, holding out an open pack of sweets.

"Shut the hell up, Donny," Gus instructed, pressing his foot harshly against the gas and screeching the car across the road.

"Rightyo!" Donny replied, again, way too cheerfully.

'Rightyo?' Who talks like that?

Gus relished the numbing silence that ensued for the next twenty minutes. They were setting off from Yorkshire, and they had a long drive ahead of them before they reached the death pit that was London. Gus knew he'd have to drive at a cautionary speed to avoid any hidden infected, and that the length of the journey would grow more and more tedious if Donny's incessant happiness persevered. He was not prepared to spend the next two days making pathetic idle conversation with a guy who has his own name tattooed on his arm and replied with "rightyo" when told to shut up.

Gus's mind drifted off to tactics. He had loaded the boot up in preparation with all the weapons he may need. Grenades, rifles, shotguns, Uzi, sniper, night-vision. Anything that could give him an advantage over the undead.

He was making no mistake about it – he was going to war.

And he wasn't sure he'd make it out.

In fact, he hoped he didn't.

He imagined himself finding this girl, showing her the way out of London. She would run out to Donny, awaiting her next to the car. Then Gus would hang back and allow a mass of zombies to overcome him, tearing him apart. He would use his final bullet to shoot himself in his head, finally finding his salvation, and going down as a martyr.

His heavenly thoughts were interrupted by a loud sucking sound in the seat next to him.

He slowly rotated his head toward Donny and gave him a grave stare, which went completely unnoticed.

The bloke was peeling the outer layer of the fruit pastels off with his teeth. He was sucking and nibbling until the spongy inside of the small sweet was left, eating the remains a bit at a time, then licking each of his fingers clean. As soon as he'd finish his mind-numbingly infuriating way of eating that sweet, he'd get started on another one.

Gus had seen less annoying eating habits in the undead.

"D'you mind?" Gus grunted.

"Hm?" Donny responded, turning his guiltless face toward Gus.

"Could you stop that?" Gus demanded. "And it's not 'hm.' It's 'pardon.' Learn some bloody manners."

Donny began sucking on the next sweet.

"Oh, sorry, is this annoying?"

"Yes it's soddin' annoyin', didn't I just tell you?

Stop it."

"I didn't realise."

He finished that sweet, then peered into the bag.

"Well, I only have six more to go."

"You what?"

"I said I only have six more to go, so you won't have to put up with it much longer."

Gus turned onto the motorway and accelerated the car to eighty miles per hour, hoping the speed would give him an outlet for his sudden spurt of anger, all the while glaring with an open mouth in Donny's direction.

"Are you fucking kidding?"

"You what?"

"I said to stop it. And it's not 'you what' – it's 'pardon.'"

"I promise, after these six sweets."

Gus couldn't believe that this kid was going to dare suck on another one of those sweets.

As Donny lifted the next one to his mouth, Gus shot out his paw and clamped it around Donny's wrist, holding it tightly.

"If you suck on another sweet, I will break your legs."

"That's not very polite."

Gus's eyes narrowed intently.

"What?"

"You told me to mind my manners, well, maybe you should mind yours."

Donny used the hand not held captive by Gus to select another sweet and place it in his mouth.

He began sucking.

"I said *quit it!*"

Gus roared and threw his beefy hand forward.

Before he could halt any further sucking, Donny cried out and Gus abruptly turned his attention back to the road.

A row of cars in front of him immediately took his attention.

Instinct took over, and he couldn't hit the brakes quick enough.

But it was too late. They weren't going to stop in time.

His brain worked quickly. There had to be a way out of the inevitable crash. There was a gap in the long line of cars – a narrow one, but big enough to fit the car through sideways.

There was a manoeuvre he knew. He had used it in Afghanistan to escape a number of landmines he saw at the very last moment. A handbrake turn. Just a little pressure on the lever, and the right amount of acceleration.

He lifted the handbrake slightly. Placed his foot on the accelerator.

But as soon as his foot applied any pressure, the bullet lodged in his calf forced him to think of nothing but the pain. His foot thrashed out and hit the pedal with far too much strength.

He'd mistimed it.

The manoeuvre failed.

The car turned to its side and veered toward the line of cars. The side of the Ferrari smacked into them and went spinning into the air.

The seatbelts did nothing.

Gus was flung about the carriage, and hit his head against the roof.

It all went blank.

He came around in flashes. At first, he felt the impact of the car pounding against the floor.

Secondly, he felt the car turn once more.

His vision blurred.

A gunk of blood slid into his eye.

His eyes closed again. His mind vacant, his thoughts absent.

He came around later to the sound of multiple zombies groaning.

8

The dull evening glow cast a luminescent dark grey over the horizon. Trees rustled with a slight nudge of wind, and rain clouds grew closer.

Still, Sadie purred at the sight. A beautiful evening sky was one of the few pleasures she could still conceive, and she treasured it.

It was one of the only things she could still understand.

A distant hum grew closer.

Her feral paws scurried across the ground as she made her way to the cover of a tree, darting her eyes back and forth, seeking out the source of the sound.

She peered into the motorway that sat, normally deserted, down a steep drop and beside the wooded area Sadie had made her home. Her eyes widened, her senses growing alert. A potential danger made her skin prick.

Within seconds, a Ferrari had sped across the middle lane and smashed into a row of static vehicles. Sadie watched with amazement as the car spun multiple times through the air, whirling in circular motions like a wild cog, and landed upside down. The roof crashed inwards and the glass of the windscreen shattered. Once the car had stopped spinning, it slid across the surface, leaving dark skid lines behind it before coming to a gradual stop a long way from where it had crashed.

Groans grew closer.

She could smell them. Reacting to the sound. Instinctively meandering toward any potential food.

She knew that's what they were doing, because it's what she wanted to do too. To hunt. To feed.

But she wouldn't. She couldn't.

Her head lifted, listening intently.

The groans grew closer, and closer still.

Sadie watched the distance beyond the wooded area where she took shelter, remaining motionless as the silhouettes of a line of limping, crouching, debauched figures emerged. They were running.

Flight or fight pounded against her skull. The infected grew rapidly closer. A safe space was needed, and needed fast. She couldn't be sure of how many there would be.

She ensured her knives were secure behind her back. She clutched them tightly, relishing the feel of their smooth leather handles, seeking that extra reassurance that her weapons were there should she need them.

She leapt onto a tree trunk, wrapped her arms around it, and scurried upwards. Once she reached the branches, she made a few slick movements that took her to the top of the tree, allowing herself to watch the chaos from higher ground.

A horde of at least twenty contorted beasts stumbled over the fence separating the grass from the road, each of them staring intently at the upturned car. Some of them fell over the separation, only to be trampled on by the stronger and less incapacitated undead, prying forward at the sight and smell of fresh meat.

Each one of them was foul. Pale, skin hanging off their bones, limbs veering off in skewwhiff directions. Despite their obvious deformities they were quick, and they descended upon the vehicle with a sick desperation to feed and maim.

Sadie's curiosity piqued. She could smell something. Amidst the smell of rotting flesh, she could smell something different. Something like...

Fresh meat.

People were alive in that car. Living souls were at risk of death.

What of those souls?

It would be inhuman for her to let them die.

She wanted to kill them too. To eat them.

No. Save them. Save people.

They didn't have long.

Without a moment's hesitation, Sadie leapt back down the tree trunk.

Flight turned to fight.

She used her two arms and her two legs to surge forward like a gazelle, nearing the mass of hungry fiends with hostility in her eyes.

Some of them heard her. They even turned around, casting their yellow pupils on the approaching warm-blooded creature.

One of them ran for her. She lifted out her claw and shoved it through its chest, then retracted it, allowing blood to spray over her face.

She did not blink.

A few more moaned in acknowledgement of new

flesh, directing their yellows in her direction.

She made her way through them in a swift succession of movements, dicing and slicing their heads from their necks and their limbs from their bodies.

One unexpectedly approached behind her. She landed her bare foot into its knee, forcing a loud crack as it bent backwards, then grabbed its throat in her hand and pulled it apart, throwing its loose oesophagus into the hungry crowd.

What used to be an old man swung its arms toward her. She dove her head forward and sunk her teeth into the side of its neck. As she pulled away, she threw the various pieces of bloody flesh from her teeth to the floor.

She withdrew her two knives she kept tucked in the back of her trousers and charged forward, venomously screaming as she ploughed her blades through a succession of the creatures. She tore her knives through their faces and ripped her hands through their bellies, leaving a line of legs and torsos across the road.

Decapitated heads snapped their jaws and chests without legs dragged themselves forward, their eyes reaching for nearby flesh.

With a few swift swipes, Sadie slashed their heads, ending their pathetic unlives with the same violence in which they'd entered it.

Twenty fast, strong creatures, taken out by one. It was almost *too* easy.

She turned toward the car.

Two men watched from within. One big and intense, the other small, scrawny, and startled.

She growled at them, holding her knives in each

hand, breathing heavily. Her panting persevered as the adrenaline continued to run through her body, ready, watching intently with rogue eyes, waiting to see their next move.

9

She looked up to her father with eyes of adoration.

Gus looked back at her.

His daughter, in his arms, hugging him tightly.

God, I love this girl.

"Daddy, can you stay here?" she asked. "I mean, stay here forever?"

How he wished he could.

How he wished he could say yes.

But something told him he couldn't. Something afar, speaking in the distance of his undisclosed thoughts.

"No, Laney, I can't."

"But, Daddy!"

"I know, I know, I want to stay too," he told her, wrapping his arms securely around her torso. "But this isn't real."

"What?" she asked, bemused.

"This–" Gus spoke, tears in his eyes. "This isn't real. I have to go back."

She faded, and his mind turned back to reality.

10

The smell of burning asphalt hit Gus first.

Followed by the deafening thump of a broken wheel making its escape from the overturned car.

Then the groans.

He reached his arm across his body toward the seatbelt, his muscles aching upon each movement. Wincing through the pain, he undid the strap and allowed himself to drop to the floor – which was now the roof of the car.

A sharp bite of broken glass stung his neck. He rolled away from the crushed windscreen and wiped the pieces off himself.

He saw the unmistakable legs of the undead marching toward the car. They had evidently heard the sound and came running for fresh meat.

For a moment, he contemplated letting them kill him. Just relaxing, closing his eyes, withstanding the initial pain, then sinking into death.

But no.

He had to wait.

After the mission. I can die after the mission.

He turned to his side, where he saw Donny starting to come around. A long streak of blood decorated the centre of his face, and his arm was twisted away from his body.

As Donny became more aware, he panicked.

"Cool it," Gus urged him. "Cool it."

Donny looked at Gus with wide eyes. His face showed sudden fear, followed by an instant of clarity illuminating his mind with the information of what had happened – followed just as quickly by an expression of dread as the hands of zombies reached into the vehicle.

Gus remained still and calm.

Donny didn't.

He winced, pulling himself away from the hands, doing all he could to stop them from even scraping his skin.

Gus relaxed. Allowed the hands to brush against his face, knowing that they couldn't reach far enough in.

"Chill," Gus instructed Donny.

He was ignored.

Gus reached out a hand and grabbed Donny's non-injured shoulder.

"Chill!" he demanded. "Relax, or you won't think clearly."

A growl announced itself clearly from behind the zombies, and with a sudden movement, the hands retracted.

The growl was animalistic, without a doubt – but it was different to a zombie growl. Gus couldn't put his finger on it, but knew it was different. Not zombie, not quite human. It was something else.

A quick succession of violent sounds accompanied the sight of legs giving way to spilt blood. Gus watched intently as he listened to flesh being ripped, followed by the slick movement of knife through bone.

Gus knew Donny wouldn't recognise such sounds for what they were. Donny would just think they were sounds of battle.

But Gus knew the sounds well enough to recognise each and every one of them.

Within seconds, the zombies were turned to remnants of bodies, covered in blood and limbs.

A girl crouched and peered at Gus and Donny.

The girl growled.

Her appearance took Gus by instant surprise. She didn't look human enough to be human, but didn't look unhuman enough to be anything else. Her hair was scraggly, twisted into greasy knots and pointing in various directions. Her face was covered in dirt and her eyes looked feral. His teeth were dirty, and subtly pointed. Her clothes were messy rags hanging off her bony flesh, dark and muddy.

She held a knife in each hand.

"Hello?" Donny asked with a high-pitched screech. "Can you help us?!"

Gus lifted an arm out to signal for him to halt, shushing him.

"Are you joking?" Donny squealed. "She just saved us! She's here to help!"

"How about you shut the hell up and remember I'm the one who knows how to deal with these situations, yeah?" he spoke bluntly in a low, irritable grunt.

Gus twisted his body so that his legs were out of the space where the windscreen used to be. He slowly crawled, keeping his eyes on the girl the whole time, careful not to make any sudden movements, edging out of the car. Eventually, he was able to lift himself over the broken glass and crawl along the ground, taking himself to his knees.

As he went to get to his feet, she lifted her lip into a snarl, pointing a knife out toward him.

He stayed still. Didn't move. Kept his hand out cautiously, staying on his knees.

"It's okay," he assured her. "It's okay. We aren't zombies. Look." He lifted his arms to reveal his body intact, ignoring the pain in his muscles. "See, no limbs missing. No blood. Nothing. We're fine."

With a hesitant glare, she crawled toward him on all fours, keeping her hands clutched on the handle of the blade. She sniffed him. Like an untamed beast, she went up and down his neck, taking in his scent.

Behind him, he heard Donny climbing out of the car. As he realised his arm was hurt, he cried out, causing the girl to jolt upwards in alarm.

"Donny, shut the fuck up," Gus urged him in a low pitch. "Your arm is hurt, just man up and come out slowly."

He turned back to the girl, holding his arms in the air, remaining motionless.

"See, I'm safe. It's okay. He's safe, too."

She leant her face toward Donny and sniffed. Like a wild cat, she moved her face up and down his chest, up his neck, and to his cheek.

"What is she?" Donny inquired.

Gus frowned. "How the hell would I know? How about I consult the encyclopaedia of bizarre shit."

She backed up slightly.

"What's your name?" Gus asked.

Sadie looked back at him with a scowl, unsure what he was saying.

"Your name," Gus repeated. "What is it?"

"…Sadie…" she whispered.

"Well, Sadie. I'm Gus. And this dickhead behind me is Donny."

She turned her wary gaze to Donny, then back to Gus.

"Donny appears to have hurt his arm, possibly broken it. I'm going to need to administer first aid. Is there anywhere you can take us that's safe?"

"…Safe…"

"Yes, like a home."

"…Home…"

"Yes, a home. Do you have one?"

She nodded.

"Can you take us there?"

She nodded again, then turned around and sauntered with a cavewoman-esque limp across the road and toward the wooded area.

Gus turned to Donny, whose face was scrunched up in pain, clutching his wounded elbow.

"I'll fix it up," Gus assured him. "Just try to keep up, yeah?"

Gus followed Sadie, having to maintain a light jog in order to keep up with her, followed by Donny, who huffed from his lack of fitness.

The whole time he watched her, wondering what she was.

Human, yes.

But he had a feeling there was more to her than that.

11

A sharp yet vacant illuminous glow lit the street. Street lamps were a thing of the past. Driver's headlights, lights in the windows of nearby houses, even torches – such things were forbidden past curfew.

All that Eugene had to light the street below was the moon. Once his eyes adjusted, the vague bluish haze of a rainy night became clear and he no longer had to strain.

There was no action below. No running, no screaming. No eating.

It was peaceful. As it used to be.

No one came out at night. Whether the curfew he had proposed and seen brought into power had existed or not, it would still be an unthinkable thought to leave the safety of one's home past dark. You would be the only target. Once an infected would find you, it would attract the next infected, then the next, then the snowball effect would continue until you were screaming beneath a horde of hundreds.

Lights were off so as not to attract the attention of the wandering dead. Occasionally, you could see the reflection of the moon in a distant pupil, someone staring out their window at what the world had become. But you never saw lights.

The infected outside meandered across the road, leaning to one side, generally the side that didn't have any guts hanging out or limbs missing.

Just one sound. That would be all it would take. Then that wandering nomadic specimen would change from the aimless, helpless creature, to a rabid carnivorous predator.

The cloak of night would conceal them from you, but it would not conceal you from them.

Eugene returned to his desk that was situated across the room. A single candle flickered, out of reach of the prying window, waving in the subtle breeze caught by Eugene wandering by.

He shuffled through a few more papers that had arrived on his desk. He couldn't even remember how they got there. Sifting through them made him bored. When he became the leader of one of the few still-standing countries in the world – that is, to use 'still-standing' in the loosest meaning of the word – he thought it would be action. Declaring war. Motivating his troops to fight.

But it was paperwork. Sheet after sheet after bloody sheet of it.

He signed off a few dotted lines, only glancing at what they were about, too tired to read them thoroughly.

He considered going to bed. Problem was, he never slept. No matter what he did, he would toss and turn. He used to read the new and latest book on his Kindle before sleeping, but alas, there were very few new great works of literature being released these days. So he leant back in his office chair, stretched his legs out, and sipped on a now cold cup of tea.

Slipping a sneaky hand into the top desk drawer, he found a pack of cigarettes. His guilty habit. Not one he would let other people see. Not because he was afraid of being judged, oh no – the world had gone to hell, humanity was far past judging someone for wanting to relieve the tension with a quick smoke. No, he wouldn't let other people see, as then he would feel compelled to share them. The number of cigarettes in the world was depleting, and he intended to keep his secret stash to himself.

He placed the end of the cigarette in his mouth, raised a match and lit it, then closed his eyes as he breathed in the beautiful taste of inevitable death.

The smoke flew out of his pursed lips, lingered in the air, then disappeared into the shadows.

What a feeling.

He took another drag, a long one this time, enjoying the subtle nuances of what his wife used to nag him about.

That was one thing he didn't miss. His wife.

Despicable woman.

Had a belly the size of a whale, and a laugh loud enough to match. When they had first met they had been young, and he had been foolish. She trapped him with a daughter, and he gave in to being pressured into marriage. As the years grew bigger, so did she.

Imagine, he thought. *If people knew what I am thinking about that dead bitch right now...*

He knew how it sounded. He didn't care. If someone was to object to his provocations about that vile woman, he would simply answer, "You didn't know her."

She had teeth lightly tinged yellow, hair that curled

into large002C messy strands of fake blond, and pearl necklaces that sat above cleavage that was only so big because it corresponded with her belt size.

And now here he was.

Free of her. Ruling the country. About to make the biggest decision that had ever been made in the history of the country.

This was beyond anything any prime minister had ever done.

This plan. It was genius.

Nothing short of pure, unadulterated, incontrovertible, inescapable genius.

Gus Harvey was on his way to save the girl. Donny Jevon at his side, probably pissing him off the whole time in the way that infuriating kid had always pissed Eugene off.

Genius.

Everything was coming to fruition.

The plan was on track.

12

An unprecedented trek through the woods had left Gus anxious. He knew they had limited time and that a girl's life hung in the balance. Whether this girl was the daughter of an important man or not, it didn't matter – her life could still be saved.

Unlike so many others.

Unlike…

Stop it.

Stay focussed.

Keep alert.

Donny kept tripping up, struggling to battle through the apparent pain of his arm. Gus attempted to put an arm around Donny to support him, but was already struggling with a heavy sniper rifle over his back. Finding the rifle increasingly difficult to carry due to its being constantly knocked by Donny's incessant wriggling, Gus knew that he was going to have to either lose Donny, or lose the rifle.

After momentarily entertaining the notion of /dumping Donny in a hedge and persevering without him, his conscience concluded that he was going to have to lose the weapon instead.

Stupid little rat boy. I like that gun…

With a hesitant tut, Gus discarded his sniper rifle

beside a tree and covered it with leaves, then supported Donny's hysterically writhing body. Deciding that the Colt .45 attached to his belt would have to be enough, he marked the tree, in hope that he would be able to retrieve the sniper rifle upon their return. He looked around him for any other significant landmarks he could use to track back to the rifle. He noticed a burnt-out jeep and made a mental note of it.

He wished he had a watch on. He looked to the sky, where the sun had disappeared and the moon had begun to take its place. This told him it was early evening, and the cloak of night would soon be thrown over them.

This was an interruption he had not planned for.

With an irritable huff, he decided he may just have to accept this delay and deal with it the best he could. Adjust the schedule. Change his planned timings.

After all, they still had at least a day and a half.

Well, that was until the explosion. They actually had to get into the zombie-infested city first, locate her (God knows how he was going to do that), then extract her, and get far enough away from the city in time to ensure that they did not get caught in the impact that such a large bombing would inevitably bring with it.

The girl – Sadie, as she had grunted in her minimal introduction – led them to an opening that revealed a house.

Though 'house' was a loose term.

It was more like an abandoned, claustrophobically small cottage, set in the middle of the woods. It was the kind of place you would nip in to shelter from rain, not set up an abode. The poor excuse for roofing had various holes that allowed leaks to filter through, had a large infestation of mould and asbestos, and was being eroded by the rain at an accelerated pace.

Gus kept Donny's good arm around him, dragging him forward as he followed Sadie inside. Donny's moaning was a continual, non-stop murmur. Gus understood how horrible it would be to break an arm, if that was what had actually happened – hell, he'd broken seven – but the idiot needed to man up. Back in Afghanistan, his comrades would continue a gun battle with the Taliban with various broken ailments and blood dripping over their eyes. They wouldn't have the luxury of stopping and moaning over spilt milk.

Gus entered the small cottage, and the inside wasn't much better. The smell of damp hit him first, followed by the stench of dried urine. But it had a loose roof, and the resemblance of a door – two things that would keep out both the weather and the infected. And that was all they needed.

"Is this it?" he demanded of Sadie.

Sadie looked blankly back at him.

"Is this where you live?" Gus repeated, with more impatience.

Sadie nodded her head vigorously.

"… Home …" she grunted, her greasy, thick hair spilling over the front of her face.

"Okay." Gus didn't have time to figure out what was up with this girl. She seemed more like a feral creature than a young woman, but right now he needed to see to Donny's arm. "Do you have a first aid kit?"

Sadie looked puzzled.

"Supplies? You know, bandages? Antiseptic? Shit like that?"

Sadie looked around herself, scowling, then turned

her puzzled look back to Gus.

"Fuck's sake. Do you have cloth?" He elongated each syllable with as much clarity as he could. "Something I can wrap him in?"

Sadie nodded. "Er… Top? … More top?"

Gus took a moment to understand what she was saying.

"Yes, a top. Clothes. That will do."

She turned and scuttled away on all fours.

Gus turned his attention to Donny and ran his hands over the twisted bones. He was pretty sure he could put the bone back into place, but it was going to hurt.

"Right, Donny, you need to grow a set of balls for this."

Donny interrupted his incessant moaning to turn a look of terror toward Gus.

"I'm going to put it back into place."

Donny pulled his arm out of Gus's reach. "No, no, no…"

"It's the only way. What, you think we can call an ambulance? For Christ's sake, man."

Donny closed his eyes, winced, and hesitantly presented his arm.

Gus grabbed Donny's top and stuffed it into Donny's mouth, giving him something to bite onto.

"One," Gus began.

Donny closed his eyes.

"Two."

Donny prepared himself.

Gus shoved the arm back into place, causing Donny to scream out. Gus immediately shoved a hand over Donny's mouth, looking through the stained window to see if the screaming had attracted any undead.

"Shut up!" Gus urged him.

"I thought you were going to do it on three!" Donny whimpered.

"Yeah," Gus acknowledged. Being honest, he only did it on two because he thought it would be hilarious.

He was right.

Sadie appeared over his shoulder, presenting a handful of vests toward him, an expression like a dog that had just brought her master their slippers.

"Cheers."

Gus took a vest and ripped it until it was one clean sheet of cloth. He expertly fashioned a bandage out of it and tied it around Donny's arm and over his shoulder.

"It hurts," Donny whined.

"That's 'cause you dislocated it, you moron," Gus told him. "It's going to hurt, but it'll be fine. You're in battle now, you're going to have to deal."

Gus turned to Sadie, finally getting a chance to look her up and down. Her clothes were stained with old mud, her face grubby, her body uncomfortably thin. Even her elbows were pointed, like her bones were sticking out.

How long could she have been on her own to end up like this?

"So what's your deal?" Gus inquired.

Sadie looked back, confused.

"Jesus Christ, do you understand anything? Who are you?"

"… Sadie."

"Yes, I get that your name is Sadie. But who are you?"

She remained silent, her face expressionless.

"How did you get here?"

Nothing.

Gus looked around the cottage, searching for family photos or something that would indicate a life. A family. Friends. Anything. There was nothing.

Then Gus saw something. A glint. Reflection of the moon in a reflective surface. He picked up a small scrap from the windowsill and looked at it.

It was a picture of three girls with their arms around each other, smiles adorning their pretty faces. The middle one looked like Sadie, except... healthier. With straight teeth, combed hair, a pretty dress gliding over perfect curves. She looked like a normal young woman, having a good time with friends, possibly sisters.

Sadie snatched the picture from his hand and protected it with her body, turning it away from him and stroking it. She stuffed it in her back pocket and stared at Gus, her expression wild and untamed.

"Where did you come from?"

She scratched her armpit, then sniffed it.

"Jesus..."

Sadie noticed Donny running a hand gently over his arm. In a sudden burst of energy, she dove forward to see what he was looking at and grabbed his wounded bone in both her hands, digging her dirty, long, sharp nails in.

Donny wailed in pain.

Sadie jumped back, surprised, and readied herself for a fight. Gus put a hand out to calm her.

Donny continued to scream. When Gus realised he wasn't going to stop, he quickly swung his large hand forward and covered his mouth.

He heard a groan.

Keeping his hand fixed firmly over Donny's mouth, he peered out of the window.

A flicker of movement passed.

Donny began moaning against Gus's hand.

"Shut the fuck up!" Gus demanded in a hushed voice. "Shut the fuck up, you're going to attract the infected!"

Donny fell silent.

Gus ripped his hand away and ran to the window, looking out.

One approached.

Then another.

Then another.

Within a minute, a mass of them had descended upon the exterior of the house.

Gus rushed to the window on the other side.

More were there.

So many of them. Rows of them. Covering the entire radius of the filthy, broken-down cottage.

Their hands bashed against the windows. Those fragile, old windows. Multiple hands, with all the strength they had. It wasn't going to take long.

Gus looked to Donny.

Gus looked to Sadie.

He had one gun on him. Nothing else.

"Do you have any weapons?" Gus whispered to Sadie.

She shook her head.

The front window smashed.

As did the back window.

A fist clattered through the weak wood of the door, revealing the arms of numerous hungry undead.

Gus needed weapons.

They were in the boot of the car. Upturned, about a mile away, on the main carriage of the motorway.

All he had was a Colt. 45 hanging from his waist. It had seven rounds in.

Seven.

That wouldn't even make a single bit of difference.

The windows smashed to pieces and three zombies fell inside.

Gus withdrew his gun.

He fired a bullet into each of them.

He had four left.

Half of the door broke down, and four more zombies tumbled in.

Two fell over the smashed back window, falling to the floor. Followed by another load. Too many to count.

Gus looked at the gun in his hand.

He looked to his comrades.

The zombies that had just fallen into the cottage got to their feet. They looked at Gus. They licked their mouldy lips. One of them didn't even have lips. Just sharp, yellow teeth.

They charged at him.

13

For the first time in his life, Gus felt like death was an ominous figure fast approaching.

Of course, he had been scared before. Terrified. Mortified, even.

He had served his country in Afghanistan as one of many soldiers fighting for their lives, in a constant state of unease. He had come face-to-face with the Taliban, who had shown him and his friends no mercy. He'd been inches away from bombs that had blown the chest out of men he would call his brothers. He'd taken bullets from his adversaries, spraying at him like rain in a storm, hailing against the walls as he ran.

But never in those moments of severe fear had he felt like death was not just a constant possibility, but an imminent fate.

In this rotting cottage, with the door broken down and windows smashed in, he felt trapped. The undead were closing in on him, their jaws hung low with bated breath, salivating at the sight of his edible flesh.

He could take one of them. Hell, he could take ten of them if he fought hard enough.

But after that, another ten would come. Then another ten. And another ten.

He decided he had to save his bullets. Saviour his

final rounds for himself, Donny, and Sadie. A reality he felt closing in on him at a rapid pace.

He screamed, plunging his fat fist forward into the face of an oncoming zombie, doing all he could not to vomit as he felt it sink through their brains like smush. That member of the walking deceased fell to the floor, but Gus was already surrounded by another circle of them piling toward him, with more waiting if that circle allowed him the unlikely route of survival.

It was no good. He had failed.

A little girl was going to die.

Another little girl.

He would be with his own soon.

He raised the gun to his head.

He looked to Donny, who stared back at him so innocently. Gus saw that look of true fear in Donny's eyes that he had seen in so many during war. The same look he saw in comrades lying injured on the floor, knowing that death was unavoidable.

His finger traced the trigger.

It was time.

"Yargh!" an unrecognisable snarl spewed aggressively from Sadie's open jaw.

In an unprecedented leap, she leapt forward and took a large group of the infected to the ground. She dug her paws into their chests and ripped out their insides, throwing their guts as a lasso around the neck of further oncoming assailants.

Gus's finger paused over the trigger, millimetres from blowing his brains out.

Sadie dove onto the other half of the circle of undead that surrounded Gus. She dug her open jaw into the neck of a nearby beast, ripped out their jugular, then turned to the next three in a movement so quick and so swift it barely even registered in Gus's brain. She tore through their cheeks with her sharp fingers faster than his eyes could follow.

Recognising that Donny too was surrounded, she dove onto another, digging her teeth into their face and ripping it clean off, driving her fists into the bellies of those that continued to charge at her with enough force to send her fist straight through them.

Gus was once again descended upon, but Sadie recognised the threat and quelled it within seconds, digging her teeth and her claws into a quick succession of charging bodies, ripping them apart and strewing their shredded meat against the wall until their hearts, livers and brains splatted against the crumbling plaster and squelched down the tainted wallpaper, leaving entrails of dark-red gunk.

Gus attempted to plunge his fist into the neck of a zombie with the force that Sadie had. He managed to create a rip, but was unable to send his fist straight through with the same force. There was something about her that gave her another edge; that gave her the quality of a swift animal swiping out its potential predator.

She was faster than them, and quicker than them. It was something Gus had never witnessed, or even expected to be possible.

What did alarm him, however, was not what she did with her hands, but rather with her teeth. She dug her mouth into their bloody bodies and bloody faces without any regard for how that blood would spread the infection through her. Gus knew that a mixture of zombie blood with his would cause imminent death.

She'd torn her teeth through so many of them that the infection would no doubt now be spreading through her blood, readying her for the inevitable change as she became one of them.

She was saving their lives, but at the same time, Gus grew more and more worried that he was going to have to kill her once she turned.

But she didn't change. She just kept fighting.

And fighting.

And fighting.

With the energy of a raging bull and the movement of a swift lion.

Her movements were unnatural. The precision of her strikes impossible. The strength with which she was able to force through them far greater than her bony appearance would dictate.

He marvelled at her slick ability to tear the undead apart. Before he knew it, he was stood atop an open grave, bodies surrounding his feet, piled atop one another. Created with such fast, blurred movements that Gus was barely able to comprehend that the fight had ended.

She stood still. Breathless. Upon the zombies she had ripped apart with ability he had never conceived to be possible.

In fact, it was not possible. Not possible at all.

For a human.

He exchanged a glance with Donny. A look of alarm and relief, concerned at what Sadie had just managed to do, but pleased to still have their lives.

Sadie crouched, allowing her panting to subside as she surveyed the room of death she had created.

Dark-red blood dripped from her jaw in waves.

Pieces of flesh and body parts Gus couldn't even recognise stuck to her cheeks and dripped down her top like gunks of red mess that looked like a child who had forgotten their bib. She was decorated in violence, concealed in the juices of the infected.

He had seconds. If that.

Gus couldn't wait.

His arm raised into the air as his gun took aim at her head.

She looked back at him. Her eyes flickered yellow. Her breathing calmed, but the brutal look of a predator stayed. She looked vulnerable yet dangerous. Like a playful lion ready to pounce as soon as it was uncaged.

She didn't move.

She looked down the barrel of the gun, then back at Gus.

He waited.

He didn't know why he waited, but he did.

God-damn it, just shoot, get it over with.

The longer he waited, the more dead he was going to be.

If he didn't kill her now, she would pounce on him. Without a shot to the head, that bullet would be wasted.

He gently squeezed the trigger, just enough to feel the bullet move in place, but not enough to end her life.

She looked back at him.

Her yellow pupils faded back to green.

The heavy panting of a dangerous fiend relaxed into that of a susceptible young girl.

Somehow, her features relaxed, and their animalistic qualities faded to something just about resembling human.

He didn't shoot.

He urged himself to, but he didn't.

It just didn't feel right.

He lowered his gun.

He didn't know why, but he lowered his gun.

She didn't change.

She had the blood of zombies dripping from her mouth. Just a speck of undead blood splashed into someone's mouth would be enough – Gus had seen it turn a mild-mannered human into a delirious, ravenous creature within the blink of an eye.

He had seen it happen on...

No.

Can't think about that now.

He had been saved. He didn't know why, but he had been saved.

But she hadn't turned.

She had taken the blood of a zombie – tons of it – and she was still standing.

How?

I wonder...

He considered.

She talked in ape-like grunts. She overpowered those zombies. She was able to do things that no other human could.

She could survive zombie blood dripping from her lips.

Could it possible for someone to be immune?

But Sadie wasn't immune.

Her eyes had changed to the yellow of a zombie. She was faster than a human could be. Stronger, also.

She must be infected.

But again, that didn't make sense.

She was not just stronger and quicker than a human

– she was stronger and quicker than the zombies. How could she be infected when her abilities outmatched them?

Could she be something else?

It doesn't make any sense…

"What?" Donny asked, interrupting Gus's thoughts. "What is it?"

Gus didn't answer.

Sadie edged toward him, looking up at him, like a pet proving to its owner that it had done a good job.

She rubbed her head against his leg. It left a blood patch, and Gus didn't mind – but he was not used to affection, however disordered its form was.

"Get your shit together," Gus told them. "We leave as soon as it's light."

He stuck his gun in the back of his belt and strode toward the windows, still shaking his head in disbelief at what he may have just discovered.

14

As it turned out, a cottage full of permanently dead zombies was the perfect deterrent for any further zombies. A miraculously magnificent disguise in a way, really – disguise yourself as the one thing they don't seem to eat.

After the initial shock of Sadie's abilities had set in, Gus had decided they needed to make contingency plans for the night. Dark had descended and, however much he hated delaying his mission, he knew there was no way they could travel safely. He needed to gather himself, rethink their strategy, figure out a possible transport – all whilst protecting themselves from the dangers that dark brought. With the speed they can sprint at, a zombie could approach you from shadows and be on you before you realised you smelt something funny.

The decision, and a genius one Gus considered it to be, was to use the zombie bodies as a fort within the cottage. To pile them upon each other against the walls, covering the smashed windows and the door that had been broken to pieces. It took them an hour, but they did it. Sadie used her peculiarly impressive strength – muscle power far beyond Gus's – to help him pile them.

Donny, with his one arm still hanging loosely in a bandage, attempted to help by straightening them once they had been lifted into position. He pushed and prodded, careful not to touch any of their rotting skin, until he considered them balanced enough to not fall.

In truth, Donny's presence had been useless, and more of a burden than anything else. But if it made him feel like there was a point to his meaningless existence, then Gus let him satisfy himself.

The whole time, in the back of his mind, was the face of a little girl trapped in the heart of the capital city.

God knows if she was even still alive.

Once finished, they all moved silently into a position for the night. Donny leant against a broken armchair, his head drooping as he fell almost immediately into a doze.

It was strange, really. Gus knew that Eugene would want contact and updates on the progress of his daughter. But why consider Donny to be the best person to do this?

Maybe Donny was the only person who would agree.

This was a suicide mission, after all. Gus intended to save that child, but he did not intend to return himself.

Once the mission was over.

Once he had taken that small hand in his, dragged her out of the genocidal pit of London, and given her to Donny and Sadie to return to her father, he was done.

He would find a bottle of scotch. Use the antidepressants held secretively within his inside jacket pocket. Maybe some tranquilisers, if they passed a vet or a pharmacy. He would place everything he had on his tongue, close his eyes, and lift his drink to the world. Toast the new United Kingdom of damnation. Cheerio to hell.

He would join his family. Hug them as they ran into his open arms.

Or it would all end. And, if he had to be truly honest with himself, that's the version of death that he expected.

Either way, it was the perfect solution.

The perfect goodbye.

Sadie took her place on the floor to sleep. Whilst he and Donny had searched out an area without blood stains, she had not been bothered. She padded around like a cat finding the right position, then flopped onto her side in a bit patch of blood and curled up into a ball.

She closed her eyes and began twitching within seconds.

That left Gus alone with his thoughts.

The whole time, he could not take his eyes off her.

What she was, was completely unprecedented.

If he was correct in his assumption, that is.

But if he was...

The solution. The end of the apocalypse. Salvation.

For everyone else, anyway.

The way out.

He could be wrong. She could be something else. Something far more dangerous.

Though he doubted it.

The way she had dealt with the attacking horde. The speed, the skill, the strength. It had been remarkable. It wasn't within the capability of a young woman.

She must be eighteen, nineteen years old. Twenty at most.

She was thin. Scrawny. Her skin clung to her bones. There was no muscle on her.

She was pale. Sharp teeth. And whilst she was fighting, her eyes had turned from green to yellow.

She looks like one of them.

Yet she had moved with speed and fought with muscle that had outdone them.

No matter how many times he reminded himself of that, it still made no sense.

He decided not to allow himself to become complacent. He didn't allow himself to lose his cautious nature.

He kept his eyes open all night, fixed on her body, watching her intently as she slept soundly on the rough floor.

Just in case.

Minus One Day Two Hours

Rick Wood

15

"So please," Donny insisted with an irrefutable air of scepticism, "tell me what exactly it is I am supposed to do."

Gus exhaled.

Monkeys were easier to train.

"You go down this hill," Gus spoke as slowly and patronisingly as he could manage, "and you go to the boot of the car we were driving, and you put as many guns as you can into this bag, kindly donated by Sadie."

Gus gave a nod to Sadie standing beside him, holding a grubby, torn sack that was once a designer sports bag, and now smelt like it was what she had been using to defecate in.

She grinned and nodded eagerly. As if she understood. Honestly, Gus reckoned she was probably just pleased to be part of it.

"Okay, yes, well," Donny stuttered, "that part I get. You know, the whole, get the guns, put them in the bag part, I get that, yes."

He raised his one good hand with an open palm, in a gesture that indicated to wait for his mind to form his incoherent thoughts into clear, dictated words.

"The thing is," he continued, "I just do not like the

whole part where the motorway is completely swarming with infected!"

With a frantic edge to the rising tone of his sentence, he turned and waved his arm at the view below them.

Standing atop of the hill that overlooked the motorway, he indicated past the frighteningly steep drop toward where the upturned Ferrari was. Its wheels had fallen off somewhere in the process, the glass on its mirrors had been smashed in, and smoke still sauntered from the engine into the cool morning air.

And, oh yeah, it was surrounded by a horde of flesh-eating zombies.

"That's where this comes in," Gus declared, lifting his sniper rifle.

"Yeah, I still don't quite get where you got that."

Gus exhaled an impatient sigh. It was like talking to a petulant child.

No, a petulant child would understand better. At least their petulance would be based on sound reason, rather than dumb misunderstandings.

"I left it at a tree," Gus growled impatiently. "Donny, we ain't got long to do this. Not being funny, but there is a soddin' girl in London whose time is running out pretty damn fast."

"Well, I am not being funny, but why don't you be the one who runs down and gets the weapons!"

"Can you shoot a zombie with a sniper rifle from this distance?"

Donny looked over his shoulder at the motorway, at least five hundred yards away. Then looked back at Gus.

"Why can't she do it?" Donny asked, pointing at Sadie.

"Because she doesn't understand me well enough to know what I'm talking about."

Gus smiled sarcastically at Sadie. She beamed back like a proud kitten.

"Do we really need these weapons?"

"For fuck's sake, I am a dead shot with the sniper, just do it."

"Thing is though, Gus – do you even care if I don't survive?"

Gus thought about it.

Did he?

Honestly?

"Do it, or I shoot you with the sniper rifle."

Gus put the rifle together and placed it on his mount, assembling it with the expertise one only gets with sufficient combat experience. He peered through the visor, aiming at one of the zombies wandering aimlessly around the burnt-out wreckages of the road, just wanting something to chase after, wanting something to hunt.

He pulled the trigger, tagging the undead lurker in the head with pin point precision.

He twisted his head to Donny.

"Satisfied?"

Donny stared at the zombies milling around their fallen comrade, twisting their heads back and forth in a clueless attempt to locate the source of the quick shot through the air.

Donny hesitated again.

Gus has had enough.

He pushed out his one good leg, knocking into Donny's calf, sending him tumbling down the steep drop. Donny ended up spinning down the slope, knocking against tufts of grass and unfortunately placed rocks.

When he got to the ground, he raised his head groggily, readjusting his vision. As he stared above him, he saw a zombie looming over him, thick goops of saliva dripping from its chin as it prepared itself for a satisfying meal.

Donny screamed. He closed his eyes tight, readying himself for impact.

He waited.

And waited.

When he finally opened his eyes, he saw the zombie's corpse lying beside him, an exploded head lavishly decorating the road.

He looked up at the top of the hill where Gus was perched.

The guy was a dick head, but he was a good shot.

Donny pushed himself to his feet, staring at the multiple undead attackers now running toward him from all angles.

He took a deep breath in and ran.

16

Gus took out another bullet, placed it in position, and loaded it.

He pulled the trigger, sending the bullet into the head of another pathetic piece of walking butcher meat.

He lifted his hand out and Sadie placed another bullet in his palm, which he loaded in rapid speed, firing another shot that landed perfectly in the skull of a zombie charging at the wuss edging forward.

"Run, you cocksucker, run," Gus snarled. As quick and accurate as he was, if Donny didn't run to the car, the speed at which the zombies could run would mean they'd descend on him at a speed even he couldn't match.

Gus held out his hand and Sadie withdrew another bullet from the box, placing it in his palm with a large grin. She seemed genuinely elated to be contributing to the mission at hand.

She reminded him so much of his daughter.

When he'd be training in the garden, or playing football with his nephew, or painting.

He had always loved to paint.

She would stand there for hours beside him, holding out his palette. Every time he needed to dip his brush in she would lift it out, allow him to dip the brush, then withdraw it again

He would say, "Thank you, darling."

Then she would glow. She would be so happy to be contributing, to be helping.

He'd never asked her. Never would have even suggested it. He wished she'd be off playing with dolls – but dolls weren't her kind of thing. She was too much of a 'boss' for that. She would run rings around the lads at on the school football team, tell them what to do, beat up the bullies, show them who was in charge.

But when it came to a Saturday afternoon in, she took no greater pleasure than watching him paint for hours, helping in any way she could. Staring at him with her adoring eyes, marvelling as the picture took place.

It was his favourite thing to do.

It was his favourite memory.

And looking at Sadie next to him, handing him his bullet, it was just like–

Fuck.

He'd slowed down.

He'd stopped firing so fast.

The zombies.

They were gathering around Donny. They were coming in too fast. They were…

You imbecile.

Those were faded memories.

More than faded.

Stained. Blood-soaked. Ripped up, torn, and thrown into the wind. Left to rot. Left to turn to ash. Left to do whatever the hell they wanted to.

Just so long as he didn't think of them.

He increased his speed. He loaded even quicker, shooting at an accelerated pace.

But Donny needed to run. If Donny didn't run it would be absolutely pointless.

"Fuck's sake, man," Gus muttered to himself. "Run."

As if somehow hearing his urging across the wind, Donny threw his legs forward and, looking like a headless chicken, he ran.

He flinched and jumped as zombies went down either side of him.

But Gus just kept on dispatching the bastards.

More and more were approaching. Whether it was the sound of Donny's feet, his shrieking, or just the smell of a sweaty night on dirty clothes, they were alerted to his presence.

No matter.

Gus could handle them.

Shoot, reload. Shoot, reload. Shoot, reload.

Sadie kept handing him the bullets, he kept exploding their heads to messy, bloody gunk, just before their snapping teeth managed to sink into the flesh of the helpless, useless running turd below.

Donny made it to the car.

Gus didn't jump for joy. He knew he had a way to go yet.

Shoot, reload. Shoot, reload. Shoot, reload.

Focus.

Don't think about her.

Don't think about my dead daughter.

Don't picture her face.

Her teary face.

Her sweet, sweet face.

Shoot, reload. Shoot, reload. Shoot, reload.

Donny plunged his hands into the boot, shovelling the weapons into the bag. It looked as if he was doing all he could to ignore the snarls around him. He had a complete three-hundred-and-sixty-degree circle of oncoming attackers, but he was focussing on his job.

He trusted Gus.

Gus found the concept laughable.

Someone trusting him.

Him.

The man who let his own family...

Shoot, reload. Shoot, reload. Shoot–

Gus held out his hand. He waited. He did not feel the indent of the bullet in his palm.

"Come on, Sadie!" he instructed, watching through his scope as Donny began to panic.

The bullet was not placed in his hand.

He turned his expectant eyes to Sadie, who looked back at him red-faced.

"What have you done?"

Sadie buried her face in her arms, refusing to look up, inconsolable.

Gus looked for the box of cartridges.

It was open. On its side.

Empty.

Bullets danced down the slope in every direction.

All of them, gone.

Dropped.

Gus bowed his head.

Shit.

17

Keep your head down.

That's what Donny kept telling himself.

Keep his head down.

Trust Gus.

He'd got them all so far. Just trust him. Keep trusting him.

It was tough when all he could hear was the oncoming snarls of the hungry undead.

The smell of decay, of rotting meat, plunging themselves toward him, coating him in their abhorrent odour. It was all he could smell. The sound of growling and snapping accompanied it, constant, desperate, chattering jaws of those eager to rip his flesh apart with their mouldy, sharp teeth.

He kept them as blurs. Vague figures out of his vision. Ensured his eye line focussed downwards, at the bag, watching his hands fill it, padding it out with every bit of gun and ammo he could fit. Trusting Gus to shoot them before they got to him. Trusting Gus so he could concentrate.

He zipped up the bag.

Something felt wrong.

It had gotten eerily quiet. The sniper shots weren't particularly loud, but he could usually hear the rapid succession of the flight of bullets whistling through the air, followed by a definite splat as the shot landed perfectly in the cranium of an oncoming zombie.

Now it had stopped.

The bullets, the splats, it had all stopped.

He finally allowed himself a glance upwards. He peered over his shoulder, toward the top of the hill.

Gus wasn't firing any more.

Why wasn't he firing?

He was shouting something. Screaming at the top of his voice. Donny couldn't tell what it was, but he knew it wasn't good.

"Why aren't you firing?" he cried, but he couldn't linger any longer.

They were coming from all directions, getting closer.

Death was in his reach.

It was a morbid thought, but it was how it felt. The stink of it grew stronger still, the sound turned into a bombardment of hunger.

He had to do something.

A zombie came within arm's reach, diving toward him. He held out an arm, tried pushing him away, but it was too strong. It was forcing him back.

Another one came over his shoulder.

He ducked.

The car. The boot.

He threw himself into the boot of the upturned car. Closed the door.

A zombie put its hand in the way, and its head appeared in the small gap.

"No!" Donny wept, tears streaming down his face. He felt like less of a man, but he didn't care. All he wanted was to live.

Using both hands, he pulled against the arm of the zombie, shoving the boot closed. The last thing he saw before he was trapped in the enclosure of the boot was the zombie's arm ripping from its body.

He was safe. But he didn't feel it. He could still feel the arm thrashing around in the boot with him, but he couldn't see it.

He hated it.

If anything, this was worse.

Pitch-black surrounded him. The feel of the rough, flaking skin of the open palm ran over his face. Something wet left a residue and he wiped it straight off with the back of his t-shirt.

He vomited.

He couldn't help it. The arm was still dangling against his face. He held it out, pushing it away from him, but it continued to reach.

Then it stopped. Flopped as it died. Without the brain, it must not be able to continue.

A piece of good luck.

Almost as soon as he celebrated that good luck, he bemoaned the bad. He could see nothing in the darkness of the boot, nothing at all, but he could hear everything. The taps against the car, the continual smacks of the dead arms with more strength than they should be afforded, ploughing against the divide between him and them.

One thudded so hard he could hear the metal casing dent.

Were they really that strong? So much so, they could get through to him?

He was trapped. Alone. Laying in his own sick, with

a dead hand beside him, and an onslaught of the undead battering against his only defence from them.

He leant his head against the side. Another fist landed against the boot, and he felt the indent pound against his skull. He flinched away.

He had the bag of weapons.

But so what? He had no idea how to use them. And what, was he going to take on a whole horde by himself?

He wouldn't last a second.

That's when he realised.

Gus wasn't coming back for him.

Gus didn't care.

Gus had a mission.

Gus didn't even like him.

Sadie, she had a point. She had skills. He was just there to get in the way. To communicate with the prime minister – and even that he could no longer do, since most of his equipment had been trapped in the wreckage.

This was it.

He was trapped and alone.

Completely, and utterly, isolated.

"Gus... Please..."

He closed his eyes, clenching his eyelids together, and prayed to a God he knew would never listen.

18

Just leave him.

Gus hesitated.

He's just getting in your way.

He would be an arsehole for doing it. But Gus could live with being an arsehole.

Hell, he'd been living with being an arsehole for a long time.

The kid might even survive. He'd trapped himself inside the boot. Maybe the zombies would get bored and eventually leave. Maybe they'd forget he was there. Gus didn't know much about zombies – they may have short attention spans. Like goldfish.

He stood. Watched as a crowd of zombies surrounded the car, scraping at it, plunging their fists into it. They were already making some progress, having planted a few dents into the car.

What could Gus do?

There were too many of them. If he tried to save Donny, then he'd die too. Then the girl would die. And the mission would be failed.

And whatever Sadie is, whatever potential there was to change the world, would be gone.

Could he live with the decision?

Hell, he didn't have to. In a few days he'd be dead.

His suicide would be gloriously enacted, and he would be on his way to the pits of hell.

Fuck it – all the best people are in hell. Maybe he'd have a conversation with the evil dictators of the past, find out what their deal was. He'd have a game of chess with Kim Jong-un and breakfast with Genghis Khan.

He bowed his head.

And what if it was his daughter? His wife?

No.

They are dead.

He watched them die. He watched them…

"Sorry, kid," he muttered, turned, and walked away. Slowly plodding down the field to his next destination – somewhere he could get a car.

He was stopped.

Something had his leg. Was it a zombie? He readied his fist.

He turned around. Sadie was still on the floor, and she was grabbing hold of his ankle.

"What?" Gus demanded.

Sadie pulled the puppy-dog eyes. A look of vulnerability that was in such contrast to the bloody-lipped killer of the previous night.

"Get on your feet," Gus told her. If she was what he thought she was, he needed to protect her. "We need to go."

She shook her head assertively and jabbed her finger at the wreckage on the motorway where Donny was trapped.

"He's dead, Sadie."

She shook her head, her nose curling up into a defiant frown. She pointed her jabbing finger at the wreckage with more aggression.

"You dropped the bullets, Sadie, it's no good. He's dead. We need to go."

She folded her arms in a huff.

Screw it.

It wasn't his job to save the world. Whatever she was, he could do without the burden. He didn't need it.

"Fine," he barked, then turned and walked the other way.

Bloody puppy-dog eyes. She thinks they could work on him?

He has no heart.

There was only ever one person who could work those eyes on him.

And when she did, she would get whatever she wanted. Chocolate, late bed time, an extra story – whatever. He couldn't help but fall for them.

And whenever Sadie did that, she looked just like–

No.

He stopped walking.

Sadie is not my daughter.

He fought tears from his eyes. Willed them away. Pushing them back in, refusing to let them out.

She wasn't his daughter.

His daughter was…

Got to stop thinking about her. Can't keep thinking about her. Can't keep doing this.

He allowed himself a hesitant glance over his shoulder.

There Sadie still sat.

She looked so much like her.

Innocent, helpless eyes. Eyebrows lifted. Watery corners. Helpless, naïve expression.

Don't fall for it.

But he would.
He always did.
"Fine!"
He turned back and put his hand on his hips.
How the hell was he going to do this?
That's when he remembered.
Next to the tree where he'd left the sniper rifle.
The burnt-out jeep.

19

It was a black, sooty wreck.

Shame, really, as it would have been a really nice jeep once.

Gus ran a finger along its side, leaving a trail of cleanliness amongst the dirt, some of which now poised on the edge of Gus's finger.

He opened the boot, looking for weapons.

His eyes lit up.

He lifted a cricket bat from the car and twisted it, examining it.

It was practically Christmas.

"Right, get in, and get ready," Gus told Sadie.

Sadie opened the passenger door and slid in.

Gus opened the driver's door and reached for the handbrake.

"You in?" Gus asked.

Sadie nodded in confirmation.

He placed the handbrake down and took the jeep out of gear, wiping the mould from the inside of the window via his sleeve. He didn't get in yet, instead running at the jeep's side as he pushed, using all his strength. He felt his right leg buckle, struggling against the bullet forever lodged in his calf; but ignored the pain and attempted to run.

Eventually, the jeep budged, slowly edging forward.

He pushed and pushed and pushed, forcing the jeep to gather speed. Its wheels turned quicker, picking up pace.

Once it started rolling along the floor at a big enough speed, Gus jumped in and closed the door.

"Put your seatbelt on," Gus demanded, clicking his into place.

Sadie looked back, confused.

"Your seatbelt!" Gus repeated.

He saw the steep edge of the hill getting ever closer.

He reached across to Sadie's seatbelt, but she hissed at him and scratched out at his arm.

"Right, you do it then!"

She took the seatbelt and tried to put it in place. As she found that she couldn't figure it out, she looked to Gus expectantly.

"Right, now you want my help!"

Gus clicked it in place just as they reached the heavy vertical drop. He held onto the steering wheel, doing all he could to avoid it waving out of control from left to right

He couldn't help but scream as the jeep picked up speed, bumping and clattering from side to side as it hit the divots and bumps on the way down. At first the scream was out of fear, then it was out of excitement. He missed the adrenaline of a crazy notion recklessly put into plan, and this was right up there with his wildest ideas.

"Right, get ready Sadie," Gus prompted her. "Wind down your window and get ready."

She wound down her window, leaned out, and

rolled up her sleeves.

"And... go!"

Gus leant out of his window and smashed the first zombie with the cricket bat. As the jeep soared down the drop and onto the bank of the motorway, the zombies became distracted from the upturned car and began running toward them.

Just as Gus had hoped.

He simply held out the cricket bat, knocking it into the heads of the zombies that passed. He laughed manically as he did, enjoying the explosion of their skulls upon impact. Their brains smacked over the side of the car, their eyeballs flew in every direction, and their teeth clattered to the floor like an upturned tub of pins.

Sadie was having just as much fun. Her nails were long and curved into claws, which allowed her to scratch through their throats, decapitating them one by one at rapid speed.

They were strong, they were fast, they were in far larger numbers – but damn, they were stupid. No sense of danger as they continuously fled toward them.

By the time the jeep had leapt onto the road, they had removed the heads of so many zombies it felt like Easter, Christmas and New Year's Eve, all rolled into one. The rotting blood sprang into the air like fireworks, heads flailing in every direction.

The jeep clattered into the side of the upturned Ferrari, the impact forcing the jeep to skid into another abandoned car and send the upturned Ferrari spinning in circles that were sure to make Donny vomit.

As soon as the jeep came to a halt, Gus was out of the car door and continuing his celebration of destruction by clattering his cricket bat into the heads of further helpless undead. There were only a handful of them left after their plan – their genius plan, if Gus did say so himself.

Sadie dispatched the rest with fluid ease as Gus ran to the boot of the Ferrari. He opened it, watching Donny clatter and fall to the floor. A zombie's hand and enough sick to fill a bowl fell out with him.

Gus lifted his hands in the air and cheered.

"Woo!" he celebrated. "What a rush, what a God damn rush!"

Donny leapt to his feet, ready to run from further zombies, then stumbled to the side, falling from dizziness.

Gus dropped the cricket bat and reached for the sports bag, feeling it, and determining that it was full of weapons.

"Good lad!" Gus exclaimed.

"I thought you were going to leave me," Donny whimpered.

"Er… Would I ever do that?"

Gus opened the sports bag and sifted through it.

Donny picked up the cricket bat, alert.

"There's one more!" Donny cried.

"Well get it then," Gus told him, continuing to sift through the weapons.

Donny's hands quivered, shaking manically, and the cricket bat dropped from his sweaty palms, landing on the floor beneath his knocking knees.

With a face of bemusement, Gus took the cricket bat and smacked it through the head of the final infected.

"What the hell is wrong with you?" Gus demanded.

"I… er…"

"Why didn't you bloody kill it? It could have got us!"

Donny went red. Realisation crept over Gus.

"You've never even killed one of these things before, have you?"

Donny remained silent.

"You fuckin' liability."

"I... I... I got your weapons..."

"Yeah, you did."

Gus shook his head. Pathetic.

He looked over his shoulder at Sadie. Her face was completely drenched in blood. She appeared to be happily licking the blood off her palms as if cleaning herself, completely unaware of the state she was in. She looked immensely proud of herself.

"Right," Gus decided. "I'm going to go see if I can hot wire one of these cars. How about you find yourself a nice frilly dress while I do that?"

Gus wandered toward the line of cars, muttering to himself, holding the bag of weapons securely in his hand.

20

One's meal is often judged by the level of silence which accompanies it.

Should you find yourself waving your food around on your fork as you divulge in some loose manner of small talk, chances are that meal is not rewarding enough for you to devote your time to.

If you should, however, find yourself preoccupied by your meal with such dedication and haste that you find yourself rendered incapable of sentences with multiple clauses, then luck may be that you have found a meal adequately prepared and executed to your liking.

Such was the atmosphere in the Simons household. Although James, his wife, Trisha, and his beloved ten-year-old daughter, Stacey, loved to engage in conversations looping in various directions, before frolicking in the drawing room whilst James enjoyed his post-meal cigar, they found that conversation was at its minimum. James didn't mind, as the meal was delightful enough that its exquisite taste could satisfy their senses. The delicate squeeze of the tenderly cooked meat, pushing juices into the corners of his mouth, was accompanied by the aroma of a peppercorn seasoning that only made the perfectly prepared main course all the more welcoming to his salivating mouth.

"Well, I say!" James declared, placing his fork down upon his empty plate and rubbing his hands over the stomach area of his dress suit. "That was rather delicious. For one to not only have such a brilliant hunted slab of meat to work with could have been enough, but no – my brilliant wife succeeds in her cooking abilities once again."

Trisha gushed as she finished her last few mouthfuls. She removed the napkin from her lap and placed it upon her vacant plate.

"I do appreciate the kind sentiments, my dear," she responded. "Though I should say, I shan't have been able to create such a tasteful piece of meat, if it weren't for the skilful hunting achieved by yourself."

"Ah, well. We all enjoyed it tremendously. What would you say, Stacey?"

Stacey wiped her mouth with her napkin, then placed it triumphantly upon her plate.

"I would say that was gosh darn impressive, Mummy!"

James and Trisha laughed at the forward nature of her borderline taboo language. She was a succinct, articulate young girl, and she knew how to get her feelings across.

"Oh, well I never!" Trisha joked as she stroked her hand down the back of her daughter's neatly groomed hair.

Stacey smoothed down the creases of her cream dress, ensuring the buttons of her elegant cardigan were done up and that the bow around her neck was still in place.

"I say, would you like a sherry, my dear?" James

asked his wife.

"Oh, you are going to end up quite amorous."

"Oh, well, to heck with it. You only live once!"

James stood up from the table and walked over to the bar, where he moved the decanter of red wine out of the way – a Faustino 1 Gran Reserva 1964 Roja that smelled divine – and filled his tumbler up with sherry. Barbadillo Palo Cortado VORS NV. His favourite.

"May I be excused?" Stacey requested. "I wish to go look at how much meat we have left."

"Ah, unfortunately, one's meat is sparse."

James opened the door to the kitchen, revealing the bones left upon the table. A foot remained, still within its leather shoe, as did a few fingers.

"I worry about eating the rest of this meat," James said. "I worry that it may presently be expired."

"Not to worry, we can throw it out," Trisha replied.

"Yes. It's just a shame. I did enjoy this one with particular contentment. It wasn't chewy, like so many before."

"It is always sad when we have to say goodbye to a good slab of meat. Especially one that has quelled our hearty appetite with such generosity."

James stepped toward the remaining limbs. There was still a bit of jewellery and loose pieces of clothing remaining on the side, ready to be brushed into the bin as another cadaver took its place.

"Rightyo," James decided. "Not a problem. It just means it's time."

"Time for what, Daddy?"

"Time for us to go back out on the hunt again!"

Stacey clapped her hands excitedly together, beaming her sweet, adoring smile up at her mother.

"Oh, when do we get to go? When do we get to go?"

"Why, right away, I'd say."

"Yay!"

"Best get changed. Don't want to get anything over our dinner best. Off you go, now."

Continuing to cheer pleasantly, Stacey rushed to her bedroom for the flowery dress she always wore whilst hunting.

As Trisha smiled at James, he smiled back.

What a loving, happy family.

Rick Wood

Minus Twenty Hours

Rick Wood

21

Dirty shoes atop a pristine, expensive eighteenth-century desk was a sure way to stick it to the establishment. The finely furnished oak polish stood sturdily beneath Eugene's unlaced, classy leather soles, beside a pile of unsigned papers that could darn well wait.

He opened the bottom desk drawer on the right. This was the drawer no one went in. Not that anyone ever dared snoop around his drawers, but if they did, this would be the last drawer they looked in; making it the best place for his most secret, prize possession.

He withdrew a bottle of thirty-year-old Dalmore whisky, twisting it, allowing himself to read the label, reminding himself how damn expensive that whisky was. From the Highlands, single malt scotch, aged perfectly – one of only 888 bottles that were produced.

It was worth thousands, except only to a true connoisseur of fine liquor; to anyone else, they wouldn't even be worthy of the label stuck to the bottle.

Once he'd poured himself a small glass in a fresh tumbler he also produced from the drawer, he lifted it to his nose and closed his eyes as he breathed in its rich scent. A slight tinge of coffee, mixed with an aroma of spice.

He placed the glass to his lips, tipped a slight gulp into his mouth, and held it there. It was like Christmas cake, but richer. A definite sting of honey swirled against his teeth and mixed with his saliva. Once he had relished its sharp sting, he allowed it to coast down his throat in a thrashing wave.

"Oh, bloody gosh," he unknowingly whispered. He hadn't meant to curse, or even speak, but the precious words had been released in awe at the fine taste of his vintage beverage.

Four loud, resounding knocks shook his office door, interrupting his indulgence in one of life's greatest pleasures.

Rolling his eyes in aggravation at the disturbance, he placed the bottle and the glass back inside the bottom drawer. He was expecting important guests, but none of them were important enough to be privée to his fine whiskey import.

"What?" he asked.

The door opened and Sandra, his secretary, stood, mascara trickling down her cheek.

"Oh Jesus," he exclaimed. "You're not still crying over it?"

She bowed her head. "The French prime minister is here."

"Perfect." Eugene grinned. "Send him in."

"Right you are." She turned to leave.

"Oh, and Sandra?"

"Yes, sir?"

"Sort your face out, you look like a tramp."

"Yes, sir."

She backed out of the room and moments later,

Eugene's guest entered.

Eugene rose instantly, wearing a wide smile and holding his hand out for a hearty handshake. As the handshake was reciprocated, he took a moment to look over the appearance of his newest alliance.

The man was short, with a large moustache and a suit that made him look like a penguin in disguise. He was unmistakably round, with a double chin and a sweaty brow. He was the kind of person Eugene would dread being stuck in a lift with.

The man looked over his shoulder in confusion at the state of Sandra's makeup.

"Oh, don't mind her," Eugene said. "Her boyfriend got eaten yesterday. Pierre, is it?"

"No, mon ami, it is Pascal."

Whatever.

"Pascal, it is a delight and a privilege to make your acquaintance. Please, come into my office, have a seat."

Casting his mind over Eugene's elaborately decorated office, Pascal made his way to a leather sofa and plonked his hefty arse down. Eugene sat on the sofa opposite.

"Can I get you anything?" Eugene offered. "A cigar? A brandy? A coffee?"

"Non, non, I will not be staying long," Pascal insisted in a French accent so thick Eugene had to listen carefully to understand it. "This meeting will be brief. I do not like to leave my country unattended for so long, such is the present situation. I am sure you understand."

"Of course, of course."

"I just wanted to meet you, seeing as we are offering

you something so big. If it means we give up part of my country's resources, especially those concerning our defence, I like to know who I will be dealing with."

"I completely understand. And what you are doing for us is a huge favour."

"I would not do it should I need the bomb, as I am sure you *comprende*. We have already quarantined Marseille and Calais, and set them for detonation on them. Our situation is not as bad as yours, I am led to believe."

Eugene nodded. He wondered how long it would be until he'd be able to finish off that brandy.

"Well, I'm glad I managed to meet you in person – if only to express my dear gratitude. We are in your debt."

"Please, at a global crisis, we need to stop being different countries and be one world. It is essential for our survival."

Survival.

Eugene stifled a chuckle at the word.

This was about survival. It had been all along.

Unfortunately for Pascal, it just wasn't his survival this was about.

22

The accelerator on the Citreon C4 Picasso felt like a soft sponge. It sent the car gliding down the dirty track of the abandoned A road with swift ease. Gus had always wanted one of these, which he acknowledged was strange – most men would crave a BMW, a Jaguar, or a Ferrari. Gus had always found such cars to be compensations for what men lacked, whether physically or in their gumption. No, Gus had always wanted a Citreon.

It was due to an advert he'd watched before a movie. He'd taken his daughter to see *Frozen*, and she had turned to him and said ever so sweetly, "Daddy, that looks like a nice car."

Since then, it had always been a car that he craved.

"You know what I've always wanted?" Donny blurted out from the passenger's seat.

Gus scowled at the interruption of happy thoughts; he'd forgotten Donny was even there.

"A cool set of shades," Donny continued, regardless of the lack of acknowledgement at his unwelcomed conversation starter. "I mean, I've had them before, from the poundshop and stuff. But I always saw them in windows of shops that were far too expensive for me to go in, and I always thought – those would be cool.

Like, I saw them on this computer game, on this main character with a long leather jacket – which I know I would totally not be able to pull off – and I thought, that would be sweet. Yeah, I'd like a cool set of shades. Would just complete my look."

Gus glanced in the rear-view mirror, hoping Sadie could exchange an irritated glance. Not that she would understand what Donny was babbling on about – Gus could barely understand it himself – he just liked the thought that he didn't have to put up with this imbecile alone. As it was, Sadie was laid down on the backseat having a nap, totally uninterrupted by the bumps and twists of the road.

"You'd look good in a cool set of shades," Donny continued.

Gus sighed. Was he still going on?

"I mean, you could probably pull off a leather jacket. You have that whole awesome action movie kinda vibe going on. Speaking of which, is it true you have a shot leg?"

Gus ignored him.

"Can I see? I've heard the bullet is still in there."

At times, Gus thought of the bullet in his right leg as a souvenir, a trophy that showed how much he had endured. But most of the time he saw it as a burden, something that ached when he tried to run, which was something he was likely going to have to do a lot of they were to be successful in rescuing this girl.

"I take that as a no."

Finally, the kid takes a hint. Gus had been wondering whether the silence Gus replied with was giving him enough indication as to how much Gus did not want to engage with him.

"A cool set of shades, though… Man…"

Is this kid still on about those bloody sunglasses?

Gus considered for a moment what would happen if he chucked Donny out of the car. Honestly, would anyone miss him?

Did he even have a function in this mission anymore? There was a faulty radio bashing around the car floor. Unless Donny could use it to establish contact, his part was redundant. Then again, if Donny could use it to establish contact, it wasn't like there was anyone Gus desperately wished to talk to. Why was Gus even keeping him around?

"You know, if you get tired or want to sleep, you could let me drive. I can drive. Honestly, I passed my test just before, you know, it all happened. It was my fourth time, but I passed it."

"You ain't driving no soddin' car with me in it," Gus grunted. He instantly mentally scolded himself for engaging. This meant that Donny would only try more, and talk more, and go on more about all the useless tripe that came out of his mouth.

Honestly, why did he save the kid again?

"Oh, wow. Okay. Well, you know, you got to sleep sometime, and we need to get there ASAP – so if you change your mind, I'm here, ready to put my foot down and take us from A to B. After all, I'm not the one who crashed us – just saying! Not meaning anything by it, just saying, pointing a few truths out."

If this kid did not stop rattling on…

Gus considered throttling him. Punching him. Kicking him. Tying a bit wad of duct tape around his gob so he learnt to keep the damn thing shut.

Whatever it took.

"I'd look cooler driving in shades, mind."

Mention those shades one more bloody time...

"So, tell me more about yourself," Donny prompted, only to be met with more vehement silence. "Right, okay. Look, I just thought we should get to know each other. What about family, you got one?"

Gus's hands gripped the steering wheel. Tension filled his arms, his muscles poised, his teeth grinding.

"Oh, crap, I forgot, sorry, I knew that they had... Sorry."

Gus closed his eyes and attempted to gather himself. To do all he could to remain calm.

"So what actually happened to them, anyway?"

Gus slammed his foot on the brake, bringing the car to a screeching, sudden stop.

He placed his finger on the button beneath the passenger side's window, and the window beside Donny's face travelled downwards. Donny was instantly met with the groaning of a few nearby infected who, hearing the noise, came closer.

Donny frantically tried to push down on the button on his side but, with Gus holding his down, it overrode any power he had.

"What are you doing?!" Donny cried, desperately clicking on the button beside him. "Come on, man!"

The zombies raced toward the open window, enticed by the smell of Donny's flesh, by the sound of him wildly screaming.

"Come on, man!"

"If you ever talk about my family again" – Gus spoke in a low, husky, aggressively quiet voice – "I will feed you to them."

Donny's eyes met Gus's. They filled with fear. He

looked back in those steel pupils, understanding that Gus meant every word he said.

"Okay, okay, I understand!"

Gus let go of the switch.

Donny pushed down on his, watching his window shut just in time for the closing zombies to slam their bloody faces against it.

Gus put the pedal to the floor and sped away.

They drove for the next few hours in silence.

23

Gus's legs were aching with the stiffness of a four-hour drive. This was only exasperated further by the bullet lodged inside his calf. The pain always became more apparent during stages of cramp or coldness. Like a solid intensity pushing a warm spike against his muscle.

He stretched his leg out, wincing at the pain of his ache.

He grabbed the petrol pump, hoping there was something left in it. The station looked as if it had been deserted for a long time. Dust blew from the top of the pump, settling on a cement floor adorned with mossy tufts declaring themselves through the cracks. The shop beside him was a wreck. Smashed windows with ransacked shelves, crawling with insects parading beneath the door.

He squeezed the pump trigger.

Yes, finally some luck.

He put the pump into the car, squeezed, then stood back and surveyed the surroundings.

An uncomfortable silence descended on the station. It was too deserted, too derelict. He reminded himself to be aware; the undead enemy could spring an attack on him at any time.

Through the dirty window he could see Donny turning around and engaging Sadie in conversation. She was laughing. Whatever he was saying, it was entertaining her, and she childishly giggled in response.

He hadn't seen her guffaw like that. It was nice, seeing her happy. Seeing her saved from the reality of her situation.

She was sweet. She brought on that fatherly instinct that made him want to nurture her. Which, of course, was a stark contrast to the explosive violence of her earlier fighting. The way she tore apart those zombies that attacked the cottage...

The speed of it – he'd blinked, and she'd already torn through another three. The agility. The strength to dig her nails through the face of the undead.

But most of all, the sheer violence. The immunity she had to the splatter of blood and guts over her. She had finished tearing them from limb to limb, drenched herself in red, then turned back to Gus as if seeking a father's approval for drawing a good painting.

"Donny, my name is Donny," Donny was telling Sadie.

Sadie nodded.

Gus watched as Donny searched the car for another item, something he could point out, some way he could teach her the language that, in all likelihood, she once spoke fluently. With a lack of options, he pointed at the steering wheel.

"Wheel," Donny slowly told her. "Wheel."

Sadie looked confused.

"This is a wheel. Can you say wheel?"

"Whe–"

"Wheel."

Sadie took a second, then without hesitation, announced, "Wheel."

"Yes!" Donny exclaimed, looking for something else to point out. "Seat."

"Seat," she repeated.

He pointed at himself. He smiled.

"Friend," he said slowly and sincerely.

"Friend," Sadie replied, with a smile, placing a hand on Donny' heart. She turned her finger toward Gus, who watched from outside. "Friend?" she asked.

Donny looked to Gus.

Gus looked away. He didn't feel like much of a friend.

"Yeah," Donny confirmed, nodding after his hesitation. "Friend."

Gus finished pouring petrol into the car and directed his limp toward the shop. The bell still jingled as he opened the door.

Walking down each aisle, he found little to salvage. The shop appeared to have been looted a long time ago, and there was little left for him to ration.

His orders came from the prime minister. The government had re-established itself. Most survivors had homes, they had plans in place to solve the country's situation – but when Gus walked through a ransacked shop with dirty shelves left to grow mould, it reminded him how much the world had still all gone to shit.

They could make out like they were on recovery, but they weren't. It was just the best of a bad situation. Things weren't looking up. There was never going to be a true resemblance of society again. Because they could bomb London and destroy the quarantined zone – but the virus still existed.

Just as he turned to leave the deserted shop, he felt something crunch beneath his foot. He pulled his shoe away and looked down.

An abandoned pair of sunglasses lay on the floor.

He picked them up and left the shop.

He got into the driver's seat and felt the mood of the car instantly change. Whatever happy conversation was going on had abruptly ceased. Donny turned back to face forward, and Sadie returned to gazing out the window.

Gus paused.

He threw the sunglasses onto Donny's lap.

Donny lifted them up, then turned his inquiring gaze to Gus.

Gus didn't look back. He couldn't. He wasn't one for apologies.

He didn't plan to live long enough to ever have to grow to like this kid. He just had to tolerate him.

Donny wiped the dust and debris of the glasses and allowed a twinge of a smile to creep to the corner of his mouth.

Gus turned the ignition and sped away.

Rick Wood

Minus Eighteen Hours

Rick Wood

24

Gus enjoyed the enticing serenity of silence that filled the car as a result of Donny's submission into a nap, and he drove idly with little distraction. The open road was his path, and he soaked up every turn of the wheels. Occasionally, he had to swerve the car for an infected, or slow down to avoid a group of undead feeding off the open body of a helpless soul. That's why he didn't drive too fast. Just fast enough not to be tedious, and slow enough to avoid any unexpected obstacles placed around the corner. The perfect speed.

Movement twitched behind him. He looked in the rear-view mirror and watched as Sadie stirred. Within seconds of waking she became agitated. Fidgeting, looking out the window, quickly shifting back and forth across the seat.

She reminded Gus of his daughter's kitten. So restless that it had to be entertained or it would destroy the house. If you ignored its movements for a minute, it would end up climbing up the curtain or tearing up the furniture. Gus never really cared, as all this stuff was replaceable, but the look on his daughter's face when the kitten sat purring on her lap wasn't.

It was just the rapid movements, the restless nature of her fidgeting that reminded him of that kitten.

Something about her that just meant sitting still was not possible. It was more than a simple case of ADHD. It was as if she needed to hunt or eat, and being stuck under a seatbelt was not satisfying her.

"Cool it," Gus calmly instructed. "You're going to wear yourself out."

Sadie's eyes abruptly shifted to Gus's in the rear-view mirror. They were startled, like she had been caught in the headlights.

"Don't you ever chill out?" Gus asked. "You know, relax, or stop frettin' or nothin'?"

Her eyebrows narrowed in a state of confusion.

"Can't you talk?"

"Talk?" she grunted.

"Yeah, like, have a conversation. Surely you could once."

She shrugged.

"You got a family?"

She looked down.

"Can't remember them?"

She shrugged again, with her body loose, staring at her fingers that fiddled with one another.

Gus sighed. He had enough trouble trying to communicate with Donny, and that guy could speak English.

It wasn't that she didn't understand him – at least, she did on a basic level. It was just the complete inability to form sentences or to avoid moving, it was so...

Zombie-like.

She lifted her top up to wipe her greasy face. As she did, Gus glimpsed the sight of her navel. All around her belly were bite marks. Scars in the pattern of teeth, wrapped around the circumference of her body. Each one of them had partially healed, open wounds covered with scar tissue, like the bullet wound on his calf. These bites were not fresh. Far from it, in fact – they were old. How old, Gus wasn't sure, but they were old enough to have been done at least a few months ago.

So how was she still alive?

And how was it she could move so quickly? Even quicker than the infected.

How was it she had more strength than a little woman should have?

And were there more like her?

It was as if she had been infected with the zombie gene and it had amplified her instincts. Instead of turning her, it had created something else, something more powerful than the zombie.

As if she was what the virus was originally built for.

A super soldier.

No. This is ridiculous.

Gus had managed to buy into the idea of there actually being a zombie apocalypse – but to start going into government conspiracies was even too far-fetched for him.

"Do those hurt?" Gus asked.

Sadie looked at him, realised that he was talking about her bite marks, and instantly covered them.

"Whoa, easy. It's okay. I was just asking."

She frowned at him through the rear-view mirror.

"You got pretty good instincts, by the way, I got to say," he told her.

She listened.

"See, instincts are a funny thing. When I was fighting the Taliban, back in Afghanistan, instincts played a big part in our survival. So when your instincts are bigger, you must be better at surviving."

She looked back at him. He wondered if she even understood what he was on about.

"That's the difference between a weapon in your hand and a weapon that ain't, you know. The guns and the fists and the knives, they all did some damage to 'em – but it was the bombs and grenades that really showed us who they were. Cowardly instincts of an animal told 'em to run, so they did. They knew then…"

He trailed off, realising he was just aimlessly rambling about nonsense, and continued to enjoy the quietness of the drive.

25

Light hadn't graced the basement of the school for so many months now, their eyes were becoming acclimatized to the darkness.

There are so many things one can get used to, should the situation force it.

Such as the bucket in the corner used as a toilet, the smell of which no longer infested their nostrils but mixed with the clogged air. The cold and damp, accompanied by distant drips that they couldn't place, had sunk into the background, along with the constant knowledge that they were probably going to die.

Laney was too young to fully realise the reality of the situation. She had understood enough not to complain about the lack of light or the potent odour drifting from the corner, but she had not yet faced the likely potential demise they were going to confront should they be trapped there any longer.

Mrs Kristine Andrews, Laney's caring teacher, understood it all too well. She had enjoyed Laney's company, with her being one of the more delightful personalities in her class. Yet there was a distant glint in her eye, blurred by the oversized glasses she wore. Her frilly skirt was becoming stiff, forced to grow dirtier and dirtier with the moisture of the basement.

There was nowhere she could sit or lie that would allow her to be free of residue, and she was starting to wonder what the point of them living was.

She didn't have any idea how long they'd been there, but it felt like years. It couldn't be, surely, but it felt like it. Daylight was a distant memory and, with the battery gone on her watch, there was no way to even know whether it was day or night.

The only thing she knew was that the groaning on the other side of the door was from undead wanderers who would pounce on them and eat them in a heartbeat.

Do they even have heartbeats?

Maybe some scientists had answered that question. Maybe they'd even found a cure, and they were depositing it aerially for everyone to self-medicate. A vaccine that would protect them, and they did not know.

Or, maybe, it was far worse out there than it was in the basement. They could even be the only survivors.

There was no way that she could be sure, so she waited.

But for what?

If no one knew that they were there, what were they hoping would happen?

The more that time drifted onwards, the more she understood staying in the basement was becoming less of an option. No one was looking for them. No one was going to find them. They were running out of tinned goods, and were being forced to ration the very last of what they had.

The options were either wither away down there, or get eaten as soon as they opened the door.

"Mrs Andrews?" Laney's innocent voice perked up. "What are you thinking about?"

"I've told you, Laney, call me Kristine," she insisted. If they were going to rot together, they may as well be on a first-name basis.

"I've finished my colouring book." Laney lifted a book that she had already coloured in, and had coloured over the same colours. The colours were faint, showing that they were running out of ink – but bless the child, she was making the best of the bad situation.

"Mrs Andrews – Kristine – when are they coming to find us?"

She was so sweet. She really was. A terrific child. But she was desperately naïve.

What should Kristine do? Tell her the truth? That they were going to decay until they were just bones?

Or keep her hope up until she dies?

"I don't know," Kristine answered longingly. "I really don't know."

"What the fuck is going on?" came a loud, aggressive voice from the opposite corner of the room.

And that was the other problem.

The other thing that may kill them.

Bill. The school caretaker. God knows why he ever worked in a school, what with the utter contempt he had for children of all ages.

"Nothing, Bill," Kristine replied, unknowingly grabbing hold of Laney.

"We need to open that door," Bill declared, standing up and stretching, his pot belly seeping over the top of his stained trousers, trousers that had been stained before they even got trapped down there.

Bill was probably the only person who could retain a pot belly whilst he starved.

"I've had enough of this shit, I'm leaving!" Bill decided, rubbing a trail of snot from his nose with the back of his arm.

"No!" Kristine jumped up and ran toward him, gently placing her hands on his arm.

"No?" Bill replied, looking at her deviously, with wandering eyes and excess drool. She knew what he was thinking.

"We still have food, we can last a little longer."

"Well, babe, there's only one way I'm not opening that door."

"Please, Bill, at least wait for Laney to be asleep."

Bill looked over her shoulder at Laney, who continued to draw in the corner with her back to them.

"She's occupied."

"Please, Bill."

He turned to open the door.

"Fine, fine!" she declared, holding his arm as she stood between him and the door. "Just, please… Don't let her see…"

"She won't see a fucking thing."

She turned around. Bent over. Allowed him to hike up her skirt.

As she watched Laney playing with her back to them, blissfully unaware, a tear trickled down the side of Kristine's cheek.

And she wondered who would be more likely to cause their death – the infected, or Bill.

26

Gus closed his eyes and enjoyed his first few moments of solitary peace for hours. He'd been dying for nature's relief, and this was the first moment of isolation he'd had, where he could stand in front of a view and urinate into it.

That Donny could talk for England.

He'd learnt his whole life story. From the moment his family abandoned him (who could blame them), to the moment the government reluctantly employed him. In all honesty, it sounded like Donny was the last available option. He spent more time on his zombie shoot 'em up games than he did facing the reality of what the world had become.

The naiveté in which Donny spoke with was like that of a child. It was as if he wasn't able to face the truth.

Then again, what was the truth?

That the world had gone to shit?

That it was never, ever going to be back again?

In which case, who was Gus to talk?

He planned to kill himself at the first moment that he lost the responsibility of finding this girl. If there was anyone who didn't want to face the stark realities of life, surely it was him.

In a way, Gus envied Donny's innocence. To be able to stay so blissfully unaware was a luxury he should crave.

He zipped up his flies and tightened his belt.

He turned, trudging through the narrow path between the trees. As he reached the opening, he paused. Something was wrong.

It was too... quiet.

Gus took cover behind a tree and withdrew his gun, gripping it tightly, removing the safety and itching his finger over the trigger.

The car was there. But the other two were not.

A clumsy shuffle battered a few leaves.

Gus grew alert, turning his wide eyes back and forth, trying to find the source of the sound.

"Gus!" came a forceful whisper.

His eyes darted in the direction of the voice.

"Gus, here!" it came again.

Gus instinctively turned toward the car. He spotted them. Hiding.

Donny. Sadie. Huddled together beneath the vehicle, taking as little space as they could, and staring wide-eyed at Gus.

"What are you—" Gus went to ask, but immediately fell silent as his proceeding question was answered.

"What the fuck kinda shit car is this?" came a slurred delinquent voice. A bloke, who must have been in his early twenties, appeared from behind the car. He lifted the hood of the car and peered inside.

The first thing Gus did was scan this man for weapons. A machine gun was swept over his back, two handguns strapped to his belt, and a machete tucked inside the back of his trousers. Gus peered at the gun and noticed that the safety was off.

Whoever this kid was, he was a fool. To have the safety kept off whilst carrying a gun was reckless. Gus concluded that the lad was inexperienced, and would be unlikely to know what to do with these weapons should he be forced to use them.

This was something Gus could play to his advantage.

He placed his gun away and took out a large hunter's knife with a curved blade from the side of his shin. Bullets would attract the infected, and Gus was fairly sure this person would not be competent enough to present his cannon in time.

Just as Gus readied himself, another voice became clear, and he stalled.

"Look at this!"

A man appeared, much older, possibly a dad or an uncle of the other. The man dumped Gus's bag of weapons on the floor beside the younger man's feet.

"We got ourselves a hell of a find!"

The bloody pricks!

Gus did not like people messing with his weapons.

This man held a gun in his right hand, with his left hand beneath it to steady any kickback. This man knew how to hold a gun. Which meant he was the one Gus would have to kill first.

Without a moment's hesitation, he charged out from behind the bush.

"Hey!" the older man shouted with fierce aggression. As he lifted his hands to take aim with his gun, Gus sliced his through the man's wrist. Taking the man's momentary lapse in pain as his opportunity, he stuck the knife into the man's gut and twisted it.

The younger man leapt forward, quickly taking the gun from his waist. Gus sliced his knife across the man's throat and he fell to the floor, grabbing hold of his neck as blood seeped through the cracks of his fingers.

"Dad!" he cried out before his voice went.

Gus turned back to the father, who had feebly raised the gun from the floor. Gus dropped to his knees and plunged his hand into the side of the man's throat, just as the wretched bloke fired his gun into the sky.

The sound of them suffocating hung in the air, along with the wings of a flock of birds battering away from a nearby tree in response to the reverberations of the gunshot.

Gus remained perfectly still. Waiting. Listening. There could be more people.

He heard nothing.

Keeping his eyes and ears alert, he reached under the car and helped Sadie out.

Donny crawled out on his own. As he did, Gus placed a gun in his hand.

"Stand here," Gus demanded. "Shoot anything or anyone that approaches."

Gus opened the door and guided Sadie into the car.

He turned and walked toward the wooded area, his knife readied.

"Where are you going?" Donny asked, his voice shaking.

"To check there aren't anymore. Keep that gun up."

Gus looked around for items, a sign of the two men hunting, or being part of a group. He checked for rustles in the leaves, for the sound of feet pattering against the floor, or for multiple tracks on the ground.

Nothing.

Just silence.

Then groans.

Getting closer.

The smell of rotting meat.

Wherever these guys had come from, they had been on their own.

The groans grew louder.

They were about to have company.

"Gus!" Donny cried out.

Gus turned around and immediately came face-to-zombified-face with the man he had just killed. The man's eyes were yellow and vacant, and his blood was still trickling down his top. Gus jumped, backing away, angry with himself; how could he not have the foresight not to stab him in the head and make sure he didn't come back as the living undead?

Gus fell to the floor and the zombie mounted him. He pushed its heavy throat away with as much strength as he could muster, turning his face away from the blood rolling off the man's chin.

"Shoot it!" Gus hastily instructed Donny.

Behind the man's dead face, Gus could see the gun rattling in Donny's hands. He'd gone red, tears were trickling down his cheek, his knees were buckling.

The man's saliva dripped onto Gus' forehead in a large gunk.

Gus needed to wipe it off before it seeped into his eyes. If it got inside of him at all, he was a goner.

But he couldn't.

The undead assailant was too strong. His teeth were getting closer. Gus couldn't hold it off.

"For fuck's sake, Donny!"

Gus could no longer see Donny behind the man's head. The bloody corpse was inches away, getting closer with every beating second.

"Donny! Fucking shoot it!"

But Donny didn't.

A machete abruptly sunk through the zombie's head, and it fell limp. Gus threw it off him, to see Sadie standing above him, holding the dead son's machete.

Gus remained still. Panting. Staring up at his saviour. Blinking blood out of his eyes.

In an instant, he was filled with fiery rage.

He leapt to his feet, charged toward Donny, and grabbed him by the scruff of the neck. He shoved Donny against the side of the car, placing his thick fingers around his throat and squeezing as he glared into his tear-struck eyes.

"What the *fuck* is wrong with you?" Gus roared.

"S – s – sorry!"

"Sorry? All you needed to do was fucking *shoot* it!"

"I know, I'm sorry!"

Gus felt Sadie tugging on his arm. He reluctantly let Donny go.

Donny fell to the floor, grabbing his neck, rubbing a red mark with his hand.

"You've never killed one before."

"No!"

"Then that was the time to start!"

"I know, I'm so sorry."

"I do *not* care if you are sorry! I could have been killed!"

"I *am* sorry!"

"You can't fight, you can't run, you can't do anything. What is the use of you? What is the point?

How do you expect to survive in this world?"

Donny remained silent.

Gus willed his panting to calm, but it didn't. He remained just as enraged, just as ready to beat the hell out of the kid and rip him to shreds.

"Get in the car; more infected will be coming," Gus commanded, shaking his head. "Or don't. Stay here. Like I give a shit."

Gus threw the bag of weapons back into the boot, opened the door and got in, slamming it shut and turning on the ignition, wishing that the other two remained outside so he could finish the mission alone.

Alone.

Just as he liked it.

Why was he dragging them along with him anyway?

But they got back in.

Sadie stared out the window, her arms folded, a scowl imprinted on her face.

Donny watched the corpse of the father and son disappear out the window as they pulled away, gently soothing the bruise on his throat.

Gus watched the road.

No one said anything, or looked at each other, for the next few hours.

It didn't take long until Gus noticed that he was the only one still awake, an observation that he couldn't help but find irritating.

It was so easy for them.

They got tired, they fell asleep.

If he closed his eyes, he saw faces. Screaming faces. Faces he wished he didn't have to watch die every night.

He resented their innocence.
He wished he could have it.

Minus Fourteen Hours

Rick Wood

27

Trusting Sadie and Donny to keep watch was a difficult decision, but Gus couldn't have kept driving. His tiredness was causing him to veer across the road, and for their safety's sake, he needed to rest.

Sadie was a talented fighter, and Donny... well, he had eyes. Perhaps between the two of them they could make a half-competent pair.

Either way, if he kept driving, he was more likely to die from falling asleep at the wheel than he was being eaten by a zombie the two of them didn't notice – *probably*.

And he wasn't about to let Donny drive.

In the end, it was a welcome rest. He feared that the anxiety of relinquishing a small piece of control to the other two would keep him awake – or, failing that, the desperate cold of the outdoors would. As it turned out, as soon as his head hit the mound of leaves he had pushed together, his eyes closed and his mind drifted to a dreamless sleep. Nestling in dirt wasn't ideal, and he missed having a bed, but he'd endured worse.

His eyes opened hours later, revealing a peaceful early morning sun that cast a mild light upon him. The clouds were sparse, and it allowed him to feel a moment of resolution. A moment of relaxing his mind into submission, until all that he felt was a light head and an empty belly.

Then the aching in his calf returned. The bullet lodged securely inside his muscle that had since repaired itself around it.

I'm still alive.

They hadn't let some stray undead into his makeshift nature-bed.

Wanting to retain another few moments of peace, he didn't lift his head or twitch his body, hoping that the other two wouldn't realise he was awake. He strained his eyes to see where they were, and spotted them a few yards away, in front of the car.

Donny had a knife in his hand.

Gus filled with alarm. He lifted himself up.

Sadie stood before Donny. She demonstrated a lunge with an imaginary knife, twisting her body to help put strength behind it.

Donny imitated her, thrusting the knife into the air before him.

She's teaching him to fight.

Gus smiled.

He couldn't help it.

Sadie took her imaginary knife and swept it backwards, then returned it to a guarding stance.

Donny copied, though less robustly. Sadie shook her head, making a disgruntled noise, and demonstrated the move once more.

Donny tried again, this time performing the move well enough to get Sadie's approval.

With a satisfied grin, Donny placed the knife on the bonnet of the car.

"Now punches?" Donny asked. Gus hadn't noticed

before, but Donny's brow was wet with perspiration. His t-shirt was sticking to him and he was red in the face. It wasn't cold, but it was far from hot – he must have built up this sweat from his exertion.

The kid was trying.

Gus leant up fully, watching with intrigue.

Sadie demonstrated a striking move, taking her hand to her side, then stepping her foot forward as she lunged her fist with it.

Donny took the stance and pathetically threw his hand forward.

"You're doing it wrong," Gus blurted out, before he knew what he was doing.

Donny jumpe and gasped, standing suddenly stiff and still.

Gus pushed himself to his feet, groaning at a wince of pain in his leg. He hobbled forward, limping to Donny's side.

"You've got to put your body behind it," Gus told him.

He took the stance, and lunged his fist forward, twisting it as he pushed his foot forward at the same time.

"See that?" he asked. "I put my foot forward with the punch so that I can put my body behind it. Makes the impact bigger."

Gus demonstrated again.

Donny took the stance and forced his fist forward, putting his body behind it as he took a step at the same time.

"Better," Gus decided. "Remember, strength doesn't come from surprise, it comes from what you're packing behind it. I was once a scrawny lad like you, and it never stopped me."

"Cheers, Gus," Donny thanked, a face full of gratitude.

"You're welcome," Gus said and, against his better judgement, found himself placing a hand on Donny's shoulder.

"I appreciate it," Donny continued.

"All right."

"You'd be a good teacher, if you can teach me, that is. I'm useless. I mean, your daughter would prob–"

Donny froze.

Sadie stared at him, wide-eyed.

Gus looked to the ground. Stationary. No movement in his body. Nothing but the pain of his nails digging into his palm.

"Gus, I am so sorry," Donny pleaded.

"Let's go," Gus muttered.

"Seriously, I didn't mean to–"

"I said *let's go!*"

Donny bowed his head in frustration, annoyed at himself for his lapse in thought, whilst also slightly grateful that Gus hadn't fed him to a zombie. He got into the car, as did Sadie.

Gus went to the boot, opening it and taking some water. He wasn't thirsty, but he allowed himself a large gulp, taking his time to calm himself. He poured some water on his face, allowing it to sink through his hair.

They were nearly there.

Not long to have to put up with them.

28

Watching that group of misfits try to coexist was like watching a classic comedy show. Like a Carry-On film. James used to love Carry-On films. Or something with Chevy Chase in.

That guy knew how to act, and how to act funny.

But those three...

One minute the big man was asleep, whilst some little rat-girl was teaching the thin, scrawny pipsqueak how to throw a half-hearted punch. Then the big man hobbled over, throwing a hearty attempt at a punch – then shouted at the scrawny fellow, threw a paddy, and stormed into the car.

Honestly, James thought he'd never get another comedy show, not since the zombie apocalypse hit.

But this.

Oh, man.

From the place he had perched upon the hilltop, he could not help but bawl with laughter.

"Why, whatever are you laughing at, my darling?" came the cheery voice of Trisha, his wife.

"Oh, you must come and see this utter buffoon. It is rather humorous."

With a happy smile that a doting wife would give to her loving husband, she joyfully strode to his side, hooking her arm in his.

"That large fellow, you see him?" James pointed at the large man.

"Yes, I do."

"Well, he just woke up from a most aggravated sleep. I am to assume the other two were *supposed* to be keeping watch."

Trisha chuckled. "Keeping watch? They look incompetent!"

"I know!"

They both lifted their heads backwards and guffawed with laughter in perfect synchronisation.

"Well," James continued, "he just showed the thinner, nerdy-looking fellow how to throw a punch. And boy, did he look silly. It was terrible!"

"Oh gosh, I'm sad I missed it." Still, she hollered at the thought.

They chuckled heartily, then leant in, placing their foreheads against each other's. Their doting eyes met, and their lips pushed together for a loving kiss.

"Oh," James suddenly thought, "we must tell Stacey!"

"Oh yes, we must."

"Stacey!"

From around the corner, their young daughter appeared. She skipped heartily toward them, her perfectly symmetrical pig tails flapping in the wind. She stopped and neatly patted down her frilly, flowery skirt, smiling a sweet smile between her perfectly unblemished, rosy cheeks.

"Take a look at this group of fools," James instructed, pointing at the trio huffing their way into their car. The bigger man was pouring water over his grimace.

"What about them, Daddy?"

"Oh, my child, you missed it. They were a most delightfully hilarious bunch."

"Whatever did they do?"

"The thin, messy one tried throwing a punch, then the big one got annoyed." He saw that Stacey didn't understand the hilarity. "Pah! You had to be there."

"What do you have there?" Trisha asked, pointing at her daughter's hands.

"Flowers, Mummy. I picked them for you."

"Oh, my dearest, you are too kind!"

Stacey held out a bunch of daisies, and Trisha took them with a face full of glee. She took a huge sniff, relishing the beautiful scent.

"You are too kind, sweetie. Too kind."

"I can't ever be too kind to you, Mummy."

"Oh, child."

James stood up in a sudden moment of decision.

"Rightyo then! Let's get in the car, and let's follow them."

Stacey gasped excitedly. "Are we going to make friends with them, Father?"

James and Trisha laughed hysterically, completely taken aback by their child's silly question.

"Why, of course not!" James answered, bending over and pinching his daughter's cheek. "We never make friends with them."

"How silly of me," Stacey answered, playfully smacking her forehead as she realised her error. Of course we aren't going to make *friends* with them – we are going to *eat* them!"

James stroked his daughter's hair back, proudly

beaming down upon her. His wife stepped forward to join them, and they shared a heartfelt family hug.

They held hands as they glided their way back to the car, their stomachs rumbling at the inevitable arrival of their next dinner.

29

"You know, I'm not completely useless."

Donny's vehement voice broke Gus out of whatever absentminded daydream he was entertaining his thoughts with. He readjusted his position, re-secured his hands on the steering wheel, and hoped that Donny wasn't planning on talking as much as he normally did.

"I mean, I know I can't shoot, but I do have some uses."

Without intending to, Gus blurted out a large, mocking, "Hah!"

"Seriously."

"I'd say," Gus said, deciding to entertain Donny's deranged spiel, "that with the world gone to shit, not being able to shoot is pretty ridiculous."

"That's where you're wrong."

"Nah. It's not even like it was a person. It was a zombie. It weren't even alive."

"Yes, but—"

"Ah, give it a rest, I don't want to hear your bloody voice going on."

Gus felt that he'd been harsh, but decided he didn't care all that much. What's more, his words had forced an initial silence from Donny that lasted about a half a minute. And that was another half a minute of peace.

Besides, what did it matter who he offended? Within a day he planned to be dead anyway.

"See this?" Donny announced, forcing Gus to roll his eyes. "You have to look – you see it?"

Reluctantly, Gus veered his eye line to his left, and look upon a chip that Donny held firmly in the air between his forefinger and his thumb that he had retracted from his trouser pocket. It was a small, insignificant square that looked identical to most memory cards.

"See it?" Donny repeated.

"Yes, I bloody see it," Gus huffed, turning his gaze back to the road.

"Well, it may not look like much, but do you know what it can do?"

"Don't care."

"Look at this."

Donny lifted a broken radio he'd found somewhere around his feet. He turned the knob and a gentle burst of static crackled through the speaker.

"Just a broken radio, even at its best not much better than a walkie-talkie. Doesn't do much. Just communicates with the other radios of its batch. The dial barely even turns."

Donny held the radio toward Gus, waiting for confirmation. He did not receive any, but persevered anyway.

"Well, see this."

Donny took the back off the radio and placed the chip inside of it. He turned the radio around and turned the volume up. The static ran through various channels, some with religious mumbling, some with more or lesser white noise.

"I put it in, it scans every channel nearby. A pretty useful resource to have, I'd bet." Donny took the back off the radio and retrieved the chip, holding it out in the air in front of Gus, irritably close to the ex-soldier's face. "Cool, huh?"

Gus snatched the chip from Donny and shoved it into his pocket.

"Hey!" Donny protested, but daren't try to physically retrieve it.

"I'll give it back when you learn to shut the hell up."

"That's mine!"

"Nothing's anyone's anymore."

Donny folded his arms and turned his offended annoyance toward the window.

For a few minutes, neither of them spoke. And, as Donny sat there pouting, Gus couldn't help but hide a smirk to himself.

"Don't know why you think you're so tough," Donny blurted out. "You couldn't even do that car manoeuvre."

"What?" Gus said, in disbelief that Donny was daring to speak so boldly toward him.

"That car manoeuvre you tried doing to avoid crashing into that line of cars. It failed. You can't do all these things you claim you can."

"I'll have you know, I used that manoeuvre a shit load of times in Afghanistan. I could do it in my sleep."

"No, you couldn't."

Gus flexed his fingers over the wheel. He'd show Donny. He could still do it.

He placed a hand on the handbrake. Got ready to lift it up just slightly, preparing the quick turn. His leg came off the accelerator slightly, and–

The bullet lodged in his leg dug a sudden jolt of pain into the centre of his calf. Moving his leg in such a way was causing him too much pain.

He aborted the idea.

He relaxed his leg, waiting for the harsh tinge of agony to soften.

"See–"

Before Donny could say another word, Gus had grabbed his collar, gathering pieces of his t-shirt into his fist. His nose lifted into a sneer and his eyes narrowed.

Donny decided against gloating.

Gus relieved the pressure off Donny and focussed his vision on driving.

Why was he even bothering with this guy?

Because he needs to take the girl back to Eugene once I'm done. Because I don't plan to live any longer than the next few hours.

His anger rose so high he felt like he may erupt. Just as he was starting to be able to tolerate the kid, the buffoon went and increased his fury further.

His mind stayed on the thought of suicide. The thought of ending his life.

It was the only thing that kept him going.

30

Kristine watched deploringly as Bill devoured a tin of raw beef. He shovelled it into his gob, trickling cold gravy down his chin and onto his shirt, along with the other stains he had accumulated since they had been there. Then he licked each and every finger, purposefully looking Kristine in the eyes as he did.

Kristine sat against the wall on the opposite side of the basement. Laney leant against her, eyes shut, fast asleep. She kept her arm around Laney, keeping her warm and keeping her close. Keeping her safe from whatever predator may get her.

She hated him. There was no two ways about it. She *hated* him.

She'd hated him when he was the school caretaker. Any time he'd been called to fix a lock or mend some furniture, he had leered over her like a bulldog over its bitch. It was never enough to comment on, or for others to notice, but he had relished his subtle chauvinistic nuances.

In truth, he probably relished being shut in the basement with Kristine.

But she had to keep Laney safe.

Allowing her to be his puppet was the only way to stop him from potentially advancing onto the child.

The man was sick.

So she did it. Whatever she had to, she did it.

She detested herself for it, but she did it.

She was glad there was no mirror in that room. For if they had a mirror, she wasn't sure she could look in it.

Bill burped as he threw the tin across the room, onto the mountain of mess they had created.

"We don't got many left," Bill declared, his eyes still looking at her with that lustful glint of satisfaction.

"We'll just have to ration them."

"I ain't rationing nothing."

"That's the only way we—"

"I said, I ain't rationing nothing."

Kristine took a deep breath.

Bill's eyes wandered downwards, prompting her to cross her legs and pull down her skirt.

Bill blurted out a creepy chuckle.

"I love it," he announced, shaking his head. "I must have fucked you a hundred times by now. I must have smeared your tits and knotted your hair with my cum. I've even watched you shit and piss, touching myself as you did it. But me, sitting here, perving up your skirt. That's what creeps you out?"

She remained silent.

What could she say? He was right.

She felt herself sink lower. Felt her self-worth diminish with her self-respect, falling into the bucket of faeces that sat potently in the far corner.

Her eyes turned to Laney. Ensuring the young girl wasn't listening to Bill's depraved rambling. Saving Laney from the reality of the world they were living in. Not having to hear the horrors inside or outside the basement.

"What do we do then, Bill? So we don't ration, we eat it all. Then what?"

Bill stood, stretching his arms and cracking his back. He sauntered to the bucket in the corner and lifted the lid. Instantly, the stench of the last few months of excrement forced Kristine to turn her head to the side and grimace. He stood, pissing in it, and on the floor all around it. He even turned to look at Kristine, smug at the mess he was making.

"Well, baby doll. It's been fun in here, but I suggest we start thinking about getting out."

He turned around, making a point of not zipping up his flies until she had scowled at the sight of his fat, spotty cock.

"You think I'm disgusting?" he asked, taking a few sweaty steps toward her.

"Bill, please."

"You think I'm disgusting, eh?"

She swallowed a mouthful of vomit.

"And how would you suggest we get out?" Kristine asked, ignoring his vulgar questioning.

"Through the door," he answered patronisingly, as if she was the most stupid person alive.

"How? There's no way to contact the outside. There's too many of them, they'll have barricaded us in."

"Well that's not strictly true," Bill said, throwing himself onto the floor opposite her, playfully poking her thigh with his scabby toe. She could smell his body odour and, even though she imagined at this point she likely smelt just as bad, it made her choke.

"What do you mean?"

"There is a radio. It's two rooms across the corridor."

"What?" Kristine replied in astonishment.

Was he telling the truth?

Or was he just tormenting her further?

"It's the room where they teach Media Studies an' all that. They have mics, radios, and stuff to transmit. I know, 'cause we installed it two weeks before shit hit the fan."

"I don't believe you."

"Don't give a shit what you believe, 'cause it's still there, whether you believe it or not."

Kristine was a kind-hearted person, someone who led with her head, didn't let anger get the better of her. But right there, in that moment, if she had the strength, she would have throttled his fat neck until he suffocated to death.

"You mean, you've known it was there all along?"

"Yup." He nodded cockily.

"And you haven't said a single thing about it?"

"Nope." He shook his head, his grin growing wider and more infuriating.

"Why the heck not?"

"Because as long as we had food, we survived down here. And as long as we survived down here, I got to plough that sweet, sweet *pussy* of yours."

He said the word *pussy* with a hot, outward breath, full of toxins and garlic.

Her body tensed. She filled with rage.

They could have gone for the radio?

It was there all along?

And he…

He forced her to stay down there.

Degrading herself for Laney's safety.

Forcing herself to endure his disgusting advances, just so he could take vile pleasure in having his sordid way.

"How dare you!" she snapped.

He burst out laughing.

This only infuriated her further, but she knew that when she was angry, she only came across as amusing to other people. Sometimes, being a sweet woman with a soft voice only served to make her a more vulnerable target.

"I say, get your little girl ready, and we make a move," Bill decided, standing up and wandering to the last few tins of food they had left.

She glared at him. Seethed at him. Filled with contempt.

"That is," he began, turning his leering smile toward her, "unless you want another go first?"

Her hands gripped. Her muscles tensed. Her eyes narrowed into a menacing glare.

He cackled at the sight of her anger, like it was the most hilarious sight he'd ever seen.

She swore to herself that if one of them had to die so the others could survive – he would be it.

He would never again lay a finger on her, nor would he touch Laney.

She would see to that.

Rick Wood

Minus Eight Hours

31

Feeling his bare shins paddle through the water made Gus feel like a child again. As he sat on the bank of the river, cleaning his scar in the lake, he felt a sense of peace. A sense of solitude he'd been yearning for over the past few days.

Gus was growing hungry. He needed energy for the task he was about to undertake. So, leaving Sadie to guard the car, Gus had prompted Donny to seek out food. Maybe he'd come across a zombie and finally learn to fight for a change. Or, most likely, he'd shit his pants, and get eaten.

Ah well, one less burden.

Gus shook his head. He needed to stop thinking like that. Stop being such an arsehole.

Sure, his opportunity for death was approaching, and he was welcoming it like an old friend, but he still had a legacy. He still had the last few days of his life to leave a lasting impression.

But who cares, eh?

Who cares what he left behind?

There was nothing on this earth keeping him there. Nothing at all.

Yet the thought of potential resolution did make him wonder what would become of his two incompetent comrades.

Sadie. What she could be. What it all could mean. It could save the world.

She took the blood of zombies into her mouth, and survived.

Yet, she hasn't survived...

Because she still staggered like one of them. Had the verbal capabilities of one of them. Had the strength and agility of ten of them. Her eyes still turned yellow when she fought.

Her blood could be what the world needed.

Only one question hung over his head like a black cloud.

Her blood could save the world...

But is it a world worth saving?

"Hello."

Gus had turned around, drawn his knife, and thrust it in the direction of the voice before he'd even realised what he was doing, clutching the leather handle and readying himself for whatever attack was about to occur.

Except, it wasn't an attack. It was a scared little girl.

Her face turned red and her lip quivered with tears. She couldn't have been more than ten years old. She had pig-tails either side of her neat blond hair, with a warm, snug jumper above a frilly skirt that bore a flowery pattern.

Gus dropped the knife to his side, scanned her up and down for weapons, then, seeing that she was in fact just an innocent little girl, put the knife back into his belt.

"Are you... are you going to hurt me?" she asked, her voice full of terror.

"No," Gus answered. "What are you doing out here?"

"My mummy and daddy were here, and now I can't find them."

Gus looked around himself. Whilst t/he girl seemed perfectly safe, he had no idea what her parents would be like, and he endeavoured to remain cautious.

"What you doin' out here with your mum and dad?"

"Well, Mummy was trying to set a fire to help cook whatever Daddy brought home. He was fishing on this lake, and then – then we got separated."

She bowed her head shamefully. She seemed innocent – but too innocent. As if her childish voice and sobbing mentality was perfectly synthesised. Gus told himself that he'd seen too much, and that he was being ridiculous. It was just a child.

"Will you help me find them?" she asked optimistically, her eyelids batting as she looked quizzically up at him.

"I don't know, kid, I kinda got stuff to do."

"But – but I don't want to go out there on my own. I'm scared that those zombies will get me, and *eat* me.!

He'd told the other two that they had an hour before they resumed the journey. He looked to the sun descending in the sky and guessed he had roughly ten to fifteen minutes left.

"Please," she begged, reaching her delicate hand toward him, prompting him to place his in hers.

He sighed.

She was nothing like his daughter. His daughter was so genuine. This girl was so… Forthright.

"Fine," he grunted, taking her hand and allowing her to lead him further into the woods. She directed him adamantly, and it occurred to him that she seemed pretty set in the direction she was taking him, despite being so unequivocally lost.

"You seem to know where you're going."

"I last saw them through here. You'll help me, won't you? Protect me from the bad people? And the infected?"

"Sure."

He sighed. Looked around himself. Nothing but trees and bushes. The further she led him, the taller the trees seemed to grow. They blocked out more and more of the evening sun until they were towering over him like foreboding giants, casting shadows over the green terrain.

"What's your name anyway, kid?"

"My name is Stacey Simons."

"Stacey Simons?" he repeated. It sounded like a kid's television presenter. Or a clown. Or a comedian. Why would parents name a kid that? It was bizarre.

This whole thing was bizarre.

And Gus was sure that the ten-fifteen-minute window he'd allowed himself was running out.

"Eh, kid," Gus prompted, bringing them both to a stop. He tried to take his hand back, but she'd gripped onto him pretty strongly and he struggled to loosen himself. "Look, I got things I need to do. I can't be traipsing all around the woods. We're going to get lost."

"Okay."

"Can I have my hand back?"

"Okay."

Feeling relief, he took his hand back and stared down at it. It had gone red, such was the ferocity of her grip, and it was beginning to throb. How had such a little girl managed to cause him to have such a limp hand?

How was she so strong?

Before he could acknowledge what was happening, the girl ripped the knife out of his belt and swung it into the scar tissue on his calf, right beside where his bullet was lodged.

He collapsed to his knees, wailing in agony, hearing his scream reverberate back to him multiple times. Tears shredded his eyes as he battled with the torture in his right leg.

He went for his gun, but it was gone. He went for the knife beside his shin, but it had gone.

She'd removed them. She must have. She'd taken them, as she had led him further into the woods, she'd somehow done it without him noticing... but how?

"What have you done?" he asked, whimpering in anguish, grabbing hold of his leg. The pain was searing up and down his shin and his thigh, spreading like fire through paper. His mind was filled with clouds. He could not form a single coherent thought, such was the pain shooting through him.

"Wow, Stacey, you have quite the catch!" came a chirpy, middle-aged man's voice.

Gus twisted his neck upwards to take in the sight of the emerging man. He was the perfect image of a suburban middle-class father. His hair neatly parted to one side, with a woolly jumper over open collar and light-cream trousers. Beside him was a woman with equally distinguishable taste in fashion. She peered her blue eyes down at him, flicking her long, neatly groomed blond locks over her shoulder and crossing her arms over her expensive floral dress.

Battling against the pain and torment of his manically disjointed thoughts, he went to throw a fist, but was halted by the sight of his own gun pointed directly at his face.

"Ah, ah, ah!" dismissed the man. "We don't engage in such unpleasantries in front of the ladies now, do we?"

"What the fuck are you people?"

"Oh, do mind me, where are my manners? Stacey, my daughter, you have met. My name is James, and this is my wife, Trisha." He squeezed the hand of his wife and they gave each other a sneaky smile, like they were watching their child score a goal at their Sunday football game. "You have done so well, darling. So, so well."

Gus glared at the girl. Stacey. Supposedly innocent.

"You *bitch*."

James stomped his brown suede shoe down upon Gus's bleeding calf, and Gus wailed in pain once more, scrunching his eyes as he lifted his head up to the heavens.

Must think clearly. Must think objectively. Must focus.

"One doesn't address a lady in such a manner in civilised company. Sweetie, I do apologise for you having to hear such profanities."

"It is really okay, Daddy. I think he's quite a filthy man. His hand was all rough and coarse."

"Well, you did an exquisite job of subtly relieving him of his weapons. We were behind you the whole time, just picking them up like Hansel and Gretel's breadcrumbs!"

Stacey blushed and smiled proudly, lifting her shoulders up to disguise her pleasure at the perfect fatherly compliment.

"So what? You just a bunch of sickos? Out here to torture people for fun?"

"No, no, my friend. We are out here for survival. For hunger."

"For hunger?"

"It tastes like pork, but better."

"What are you on about?"

James bent down, a smile widening across his face.

"Did you now the average human adult provides thirty kilograms of food?" James looked up and down Gus's body as if he was mentally addressing a beautiful woman. A dollop of drool appeared from the corner of his mouth. "And with you, I imagine we'll be packing even more meat than that."

Gus felt a lump of sick come to his mouth. The pain was constant, an ongoing discomfort seizing at the base of his leg – but the dawn of realisation as he listened to this man's words was even more painful.

"You what?"

"My new friend, you are going to last us for weeks."

32

Donny peered over the horizon, watching the amber glow of the setting sun.

Gus had been very precise in how to recognise what time it was according to the level of the sun in the sky – specifically, how to tell when it had been an hour. In all honesty, Donny had understood very little, but didn't want to let that on; so he'd nodded along, all the time keeping his plastic wrist watch hidden behind his back.

An hour. Gus had been very strict. Very adamant.

"An hour, you 'ear me? Not an hour ten minutes, not an hour five, not even an hour and thirty friggin' seconds – an hour."

Gus's words, however inaccurately recollected, rung around Donny's mind.

It had been more than an hour.

This only confirmed one of two things.

Either Gus was dead, or…

No, that was the only thing it confirmed. Gus was dead.

Though Donny found it difficult to imagine how someone of Gus's capabilities would end up dead on a trip to the lake to wash – something he was incredibly grateful for, as Gus's odour was getting more poignant than Sadie's, and Gus's hostile temperament led Donny to believe that he would not welcome some delicately phrased astute observations that hinted at his need to wash.

Donny recollected stopping at this service station a few times as a child. It didn't look the same. The busy car park and thriving shops were no more; replaced by a mass of burnt-out cars smashed together and abandoned, looted buildings. Even so, he was still filled with a sense of nostalgia as he reminisced over fond memories of running to the nearby lake as a child.

Donny turned to the car. Sadie laid across the backseat. Her eyes were fastened shut, her thumb held peacefully in her mouth, and her breathing was deep enough to indicate she was in a sound slumber.

Donny did not want to disturb her. Partly as she had been agitated for last part of the journey and she needed rest – but mostly as he was scared of what she would do to him if he woke her up. He once accidentally woke his ex-girlfriend's cat up, and she had pounced upon him and gnawed on his arm, leaving teeth imprints for weeks. Sadie, being far thriftier, could well break his arm off.

No, he would go to the lake, see what was going on. It was five minutes away. He would be in either running distance of Sadie in the car, or Gus at the lake. He'd be fine.

But he'd take a gun.

Seemed like a good idea.

Not that he had balls enough to use it: that had already been highlighted. He couldn't even shoot a zombie.

He dropped his eyes to the floor and shook his head.

He felt pathetic. All that time shooting zombies on a video game, but when it came to the real thing, it felt far different pointing a barrel at a real head, alive or undead.

He sighed. Should he take a gun?

Screw it.

He opened the boot and sifted through the sports bag containing all the weapons. He found a small handgun. He wasn't sure why, but it felt most right that he took this, instead of any of the bigger or more powerful-looking guns.

Maybe if it felt like less of a gun, he'd be better at shooting it.

He lifted the gun up and aimed at a distant road sign. It was heavy. Like, really heavy. How could something so small be so heavy?

Was it even loaded?

He rotated the gun, looking to see if it was loaded, until he realised he had no idea whatsoever what he was looking for. Was it a clip in the handle – a magazine, is that what they call it? Or was it a six shooter, like in a western.

No idea.

Just point, pull the trigger, and hope for the best.

Dropping the gun to his side, he scanned the area around him,and edged toward the opening to the woods.

Suddenly, he felt afraid.

He hadn't felt it standing beside the car. If anything came at him, he'd see it, and he'd be able to get in the car and alert Sadie in time for her to stop it for him.

But now he was on his own.

He paused.

Should he turn back?

He looked over his shoulder at the car. Should he really leave Sadie alone? Would she be safe?

He scoffed.

Who was he kidding?

How would she be any safer with him there?

Donny checked his watch. Another ten minutes had passed, and Gus still hadn't appeared.

Constantly scanning the surroundings, he approached the woods, staying low, like he'd hit the crouch button on the computer game and couldn't figure out how to undo it.

But this was no computer game.

As he was about to find out.

33

"You tellin' me, you lot are a bunch of cannibals?"

James scrunched his face up in disgust, turning away and mimicking a wretch.

"Oh, my," he said, like someone had just been incredibly rude at a dinner party. "You wash your potty mouth out, mister!"

James kept the gun focussed on Gus's head.

Gus looked over his shoulder at Stacey. As he was on his knees, she was about eye level with him, but her eyes gave no recognition of the abnormality of the situation. She smiled back at him and turned her eyes dotingly toward her parents. She was so prim, so proper, this whole thing just felt like a bizarre dream.

"So what, you gonna shoot me then chop me up?"

"I don't know, being honest with you. Trisha, how should we do this one? I mean, that last fellow we shot in the head, and that ruined a whole load of the meat. Stacey always loves the brains."

"I do." Stacey nodded, a sweet, beaming smile delighting her face with virtuous joy. "I do, I do really love the brains."

"Shit, the world ends and it brings out all the fuckin' crazies."

James lifted his hand back and smacked the end of

his gun into the base of Gus's skull. Gus fell onto his front, squinting in pain, the world spinning dizzily around him.

"Once again, I am going to remind you to mind your filthy tongue in front of my daughter!" James demanded, showing the first sign of genuine hostility he'd shown since he'd begun this incessantly sadistic tirade.

"Right then," Gus coughed, pushing himself to his knees. "You gonna eat me, get on with it. I ain't got all day."

"I say the knife," Trisha decided, withdrawing Gus's large hunter's knife with the curved blade. "The bottom of the spine. That way he'll paralyse but stay alive. He won't be able to move and wriggle away, which means we can keep him alive longer, and always have fresh meat."

James's jaw dropped open in astonishment. "What a gosh-darn wonderful idea! My wife," he directed at Gus, "can you believe it? I mean, she spends so much time looking pretty I forget there's one smart head on those shoulders too!"

I must be on acid.

Gus searched for something near him, something he could use as a weapon, a way to fight. A large rock, maybe, or a loose blade on one of them he could grab. Maybe he could take the daughter hostage. Threaten her until they submitted.

Then again, the daughter may be the most sadistic of the lot.

No. He was surrounded. There were three of them. The fight was falling out of him.

But what about his daughter?

No. That's not right.

What about *Eugene's* daughter?

Laney.

There I go again. It's not my daughter. My daughter is…

A bush moved in the distance. Something was there.

Some*one* was there.

Gus kept his head lowered, not wanting to draw attention to it, but kept his eyes up.

The flicker of messy hair. A scruffy collar.

Donny.

It was Donny.

"Come on," Gus whispered, urging Donny to make a move.

Donny, the man who hadn't even been able to kill a zombie.

He was done for.

"Right," James decided. "One does have places to be. Let's get to it."

James took the blade from his wife's hands and gave her an affectionate kiss on the cheek, whispering something undoubtedly romantic in her ear.

Gus's hands scrunched up, digging into the earth, grasping tufts of grass.

James moved to the back of Gus, readying his knife hand.

"Don't move!" came a weak cry, and Donny burst out from behind the bushes, pointing a trembling gun at James.

Fucking idiot.

Gus couldn't have been more disappointed.

Donny was disguised. Under cover. Unnoticed.

He had a perfect vantage point to take the shot.

Now they were just going to get his gun off him and shoot Donny too. Maybe eat him for dessert, who knows.

"I mean, or I'll shoot you," Donny persisted with minimal conviction.

James paused, dropping the knife and lifting his hands up. The one advantage Donny did have was that they did not know how inept he was. For all they knew, he'd be able pinpoint all their heads in three quick successive shots. Until they realised how incapable he actually was, they would likely retain caution.

"Shoot them," Gus grunted.

Donny edged forward, his gun buckling so hard between his two hands that Gus was amazed the kid didn't drop it.

"Please, just shoot them," Gus urged.

The opportunity was growing smaller by the second.

James was already exchanging a glance with his wife and daughter, formulating a subconscious plan. They had been able to gather their thoughts and they were edging away from each other.

Stacey was getting closer to Gus so that the shot wouldn't be risked in her direction. James was edging further to the left, and Trisha to the right. Gus recognised this as a tactic he'd employ – widening the space between the targets, meaning that if Donny took a shot at one of them, the other would have the opportunity to intervene and wrestle the gun from him.

"I – I – don't move!"

"Donny, fucking shoot them!"

Donny's finger poised over the trigger. He pointed it at James. Took aim.

And failed.

Backed down.

Dropped the gun to his side.

Sweat trickled down his cheek. He wiped the perspiration from his forehead.

He'd bottled it.

34

Gus's eyes were fixed on the gun hanging by Donny's side, gripped in his hand but loosely swinging, like a child with their favourite doll.

He bowed his head, closing his eyes, filling with disappointment.

This was Donny's opportunity.

The point where Donny could have proven his worth.

Where he could have redeemed his past failures. And all he had to do was kill a family of cannibals about to kill and eat Gus.

James and Trisha exchanged a knowing look, as if they had somehow expected this little boy to let Gus down.

They moved back toward each other, removing the gap they had created, and walked toward Donny.

"It's okay, my friend," James told Donny. "Just give me the gun and this will all be fine."

"Give you the gun?" Donny repeated.

He lifted the gun in his shaking hands.

No, Donny.

Gus willed him to be stronger.

Gus willed him not to relinquish the only chance they had.

"That's it," James continued, standing beside his wife, now just yards from Donny. "Just hand it to me."

"Okay," Donny confirmed. "I will."

James held out his hand.

Donny pointed the gun at James's head and shot him in the face. His skull blew into pieces that scattered over the bushes and trees, and his headless body fell to the floor.

Before Gus could catch his breath, Donny turned to Trisha and shot. She was already running away, meaning his elusive aim was unlikely to hit her, but a bullet did manage to skim her shoulder

"No!" Stacey screamed out. "Mommy! Daddy!"

Stacey looked to Donny with eyes of fake demented terror.

Donny aimed at the girl.

But he couldn't. Not a child.

"Allow me." Gus stood, snatched the gun from Donny's hand, and pointed it at the girl.

"You wouldn't shoot an innocent little girl. Would you, mister?"

She pulled the best puppy-dog eyes Gus had ever seen.

Gus blew three rounds into her chest, each one shoving her further back until she fell onto the floor.

He aimed at Trisha, but she had already disappeared into the distance.

Gus immediately turned his attention to Donny.

"What the hell was that?" he demanded, not knowing whether to feel aggrieved or relieved.

"They were standing too far apart," Donny admitted. "I needed them to get closer."

Gus smirked. For what must be the first time in

months, he felt a smile spread from cheek to cheek.

"You are full of surprises. Ain't you, kid?"

Donny looked to the bodies slumped on the floor.

"Come on," Gus instructed Donny, "If any infected heard the gunshots, they'd be on their way by now."

Gus charged through the bushes, pushing them out of the way. He stopped once he realised he was alone.

He edged back to the opening, where Donny still absently stood.

"Hey, Donny, come on!"

Donny couldn't move.

Gus marched back to Donny's side and grabbed his arm, trying to turn him around. He wouldn't budge.

"What are you doing?" he interrogated.

"I did this..." Donny asked.

Tears cascaded down Donny's cheeks.

"You had to, mate."

"I did this. I ki – I actually... I can't believe I..."

"You what?"

"I ki – I ki –"

"You killed them, Donny. You need to say it."

Donny shook his head.

Gus could hear distant snarls growing closer.

"Say it, kid, or you ain't ever going to be able to move."

"I can't..."

"Hear that sound? That's a horde coming this way. We need to go."

Donny covered his face.

Gus grabbed hold of Donny's arms and threw them aside. Donny's eyes were scrunched closed, so Gus smacked him around the face to force them to open.

"Look at me!"

Donny did as he was told.

"Repeat after me. I killed them."

"No."

"Do it!"

Donny looked deep into Gus's eyes, seeing his resolve, his adamant determination that Donny would verbalise what he did. Donny knew he needed to. He could hear them getting closer. He knew they weren't far away.

"I…"

"Yes, that's it."

"I killed them, Gus."

"Yeah." Gus nodded. Donny went to look away, but Gus lifted his head by the chin, forcing Donny to look into his eyes. "You did. You fuckin' killed them. An' I'm grateful for it. 'Cause if you didn't, I'd be dead, and so would you. You did the right thing."

"I did?"

"Yes. Now move your feet."

Gus grabbed hold of Donny's arm and dragged him forward with enough strength that he couldn't have stayed rooted to the spot if he'd tried to. He dragged him away, forcing him through the wooded area.

Eventually, Donny's legs began shuffling. Gus was able to loosen his grip, then remove his arm entirely. He kept listening to Donny's behind him, keeping pace, until they reached the car.

35

They drove in silence for longer than Donny could account for. His head leant against the window, watching the barren wastelands and deserted charcoal houses go by. Barely twenty seconds would go without them shooting past an upturned car, an abandoned, broken-down house, or a mutilated corpse.

He was almost becoming used to the sight. An hour previous and the thought of death filled him with dread. Now he had taken a life, he simply looked upon the bodies as unfortunate souls. Their faces were ripped apart, their brains bursting through their eye sockets, intestines spilling out of ripped skin – their way of going out was far better than those he had stolen lives from, and that was the way he had to look at it.

He initially couldn't move. Just watching the bodies slump helplessly onto the floor, not getting back up again. He had waited, expecting them to retaliate, to jump up and march toward him and beat him to death as an act of impotent revenge.

They didn't.

They just stayed there, on the floor – a mother fleeing from a father and daughter, falling over each other's bodies.

Gus had to drag him away.

Donny had wanted to leave, had wanted to escape the sight, run away from what he'd done. He had willed Gus to throw him over his shoulder and take him kicking and screaming out of there.

But hadn't been able to move.

His legs had felt like lead, as if heavy weights were attached to his ankles by thick rope. He wanted to be sick, yet at the same time, found his stomach empty.

People were dead.

Because of him.

He closed his eyes. There they were again.

"It was six months ago," Gus spoke, suddenly interrupting Donny's mental monologue.

"What?"

"It was six months ago, and it was just after the infection, or whatever it is, had hit. The whole of London turned to bedlam. I didn't know what was going on, what was happening, whether it was just there, the whole country, I did not know. All I knew was what my instinct told me, and it told me it was bad, and I had to hurry, I had to…"

Donny focussed intently on Gus. He studied the contours of his face, only to find an expression he had not seen in him before. Gus didn't turn and look at Donny, he kept his eyes fixed on the road ahead of him. One could be fooled into thinking that this was to drive safely, but Donny knew better.

"Had to what?" Donny asked.

"Had to… get back to my family." His eyes flicked downwards momentarily, then he readjusted his vision back to the road ahead. "I had to get back to my wife. Get back to my daughter."

Donny looked over his shoulder at Sadie, who had

woken up and leant forward. Even with the poor grasp she appeared to have on the English language, the emotions engraved across Gus's face were enough to intrigue her subdued attention.

"So that's what I did," Gus continued. "My leg was killing, the bullet lodged in it, it kept me limping. But if it weren't for that damn bullet, I'd have still been in Afghanistan, and would have been nowhere near my family, and would have stood no chance at helping them. Hell, I don't even know if the troops over there know what's going on. It was the only time I felt grateful for being discharged. It had felt like such a disgrace, but in that moment, in that quick, fiery thought, I felt like it was a gift from God."

Gus snorted.

"A gift from God, eh? How pathetic is that. If anything, the only thing this shit has done has either confirmed that there is no God, or if there is, he is an arsehole who needs a good swift punch in the face."

He wiped his hands through his hair, keeping his eyes glued ahead.

Donny said nothing.

"I didn't realise at the time that London was turning into the cesspit of it all, but I knew it was going to be quarantined, and I knew I hadn't long to get them out. I had contacts in the army that may have let me through the edge of the city, but that meant nothing without my family with me. So I got on the motorbike, I raced back, but they... They were..."

Gus thumped the steering wheel. In a sudden burst of aggression his face turned to a rabid snarl, then abruptly morphed back to inconsolable anguish.

Donny didn't move his eyes away from Gus's. He

was transfixed.

Gus slowed the car down, gradually, until it came to a full halt. He put the handbrake on, switched off the engine, and sat still. He stared at a spot on the road and did not remove his eyes from it.

"They were already there. So many of them. They had filled my house. I could see my neighbours as I passed them, I could see them fighting, I could see them dying, but worst of all – I could see those bastards, those… *fuckers* – charging my house."

He dropped his head, still not turning his head toward Donny or Sadie. Still keeping his eyes staring anywhere but them.

"I got in, I killed a load, but – but it was too late. My wife, and my daughter, they were already…"

Gus lifted his head, turning it slightly toward Donny, but still staring at the ground, still unable to lift his eyes.

"My wife had even ripped the legs off of my daughter. *Our* daughter."

A difficult silence lingered in the air for a few seconds.

"I killed them. I had to. I couldn't let them live. So I killed them. I got my gun, and I shot the undead walking corpses of my wife, and my daughter, in the face."

"My God…" Donny whispered.

"Yeah. So when you hesitate about killing a zombie, or a – a fuckin' cannibal – you just remember what world we live in now. A world where I – where a guy must kill his own family for their own good. Because he can't stand to see them eat other families. Then you tell him he needs to cheer up, that he's too ill-tempered, that he should drink less; you tell that broken man that—"

He paused. Lifted his head. Ran his hands over his face and through his hair.

He turned toward Donny and looked him in the eyes.

"Would you mind driving the last hour? I need a kip."

"You want me to drive?" Donny asked.

"Yeah."

Gus got out of the car and walked around to Donny's side, waiting for him to get out.

Donny did. He took the steering wheel and drove slow and steady for the final sixty minutes, allowing Gus to sit with his eyes closed.

And for the first time in a while, Gus didn't scream or cry out. He just slept.

Minus Four Hours

Rick Wood

36

A lonely raindrop planted itself upon the faded scars of Gus's forehead, prompting a vague flicker from his closed eyelids.

The open window no longer gave him the aerodynamic wind resistance that indicated they were moving, and he assumed that they had either arrived at London, or they had encountered a problem.

"What's going on?" he grunted. "We there?"

He groggily turned his head, rubbing his fists over his eyes. He grew irritated at the lack of response to his question and sat up, waiting for the blurs to fade from his vision and the inside of the car to return to clarity.

As he turned to his side, he noticed an empty driver's seat, and there was no companion nestled in the backseat.

"What the–"

Lifting his head, he noticed two figures standing a few yards away, completely still. One could be mistaken for believing they were two waxwork models, such was their lack of movement, except for their unmistakably thin, scrawny bodies.

Gus kicked the car door open and stumbled out, his nestled bullet sending a shooting pain up and down his leg.

"Fuck," he muttered. Despite the bullet being lodged in his body for so long now, the awkward pain still took him by surprise. After stretching his leg out, he managed to limp toward the backs of Sadie and Donny, both stood upon a grassy verge next to a short, steep slope.

"What the hell? I thought you'd at least wake me when we got–"

The reason for their stillness and shock became instantly apparent.

"Jesus Christ," he gasped.

Down the steady slope of the verge they stood upon was a wired fence. Behind that was a large brick wall that read the words:

DANGER
Quarantine Zone
DO NOT ENTER under any circumstance

This sign was large, in white bold writing over a thick red background, repeated every few metres across the wall.

Do not enter under any circumstance, it read.

Gus coughed up a laugh.

"Ironic, ennit?"

But the other two still didn't answer.

As Gus's eye line lifted, their silence became justified.

His jaw fell open. He attempted to find the words, but just opened his mouth to inaudible sounds. Incoherent syllables spewed out from between his lips in a hazy stutter, verbalising the disjointed ramblings of his manic, fragmented thoughts.

The smell hit him first. The overwhelming scent of death. Decay mixed with rotting flesh, hovering toward them across a foggy smoke, filling the air like a toxic spill. Aggravated groans joined the despondent howls, mumbling below the repeated smack of thousands of the infected packed against a solid wall.

They went on as far as the eye could see. It was almost impossible to distinguish one zombie from another, such was the mass of them. The stronger, more recently deceased clambered atop the weaker, crumbling bodies. Their faces melded into one greyish pale mass, with streaks of dried blood encased upon dirty rags that fell off bony, sickening bodies.

The wall carried on for a broad circular distance, disappearing around the corner to their left and their right. As far as the radius went, the undead continued to batter against it.

Gus attempted to peer into the distance, to look for the end of the masses of ravenous hungry corpses – but there was none. They did not end.

He finally understood why Eugene had decided to lay bombs upon this vicinity as immediately as possible. It was the survival of the barely fittest, the battering of the less decayed against the less vile.

How the fuck am I going to get into that?

"Right," Gus said, once he realised they had been stood agape for longer than he was prepared to acknowledge. "Ideas, anybody?"

Donny's head slowly rotated toward him. Severe, disturbed confusion stuck to his face as if someone had glued some deformed expression upon him.

"Ideas?"

"Yeah. I mean, you know, once we figure out where

we're actually finding this girl."

"You mean, you don't even know where to find her?"

Gus went to react aggressively; then it occurred to him that it was a pertinently valid question.

"I just, kinda, thought I'd wing it."

"Well, not being funny, but I don't think we could just set Sadie in there and unleash her. That's too many even for her."

"That's too many even for a soddin' army. How we supposed to deal with that?"

Gus turned to Sadie. This would be a really good time for her to start talking.

She shook her head vigorously.

"Zombies, big!" she barked.

Gus nodded, wishing she had something more constructive to add.

"Lots," she persisted. "In there – death."

Gus nodded again, wishing she hadn't added anything at all.

"Well. If this is how I'm going to go out, it's how I'm going to go out."

Gus charged to the boot of the car, wiping perspiration from his forehead. He had no idea what he was going to do once he had loaded himself with weapons, but he was used to winging it. Maybe if he got himself ready, an idea would present itself.

He took a number of grenades, attaching them to the inside of his jacket. He slid ammo diagonally over his shoulder, a machine gun over his back, two Uzis on his belt, and a knife with a large, curved blade beside his one good shin.

"You don't really mean that, do you?" Donny

appeared at Gus's side, making him jump.

"What?"

"What you said about going out. I mean, after what you told me... You want to live, right?"

Gus smiled at Donny. Not grinned, not smirked – smiled.

"You're young, kid," he said.

"I'm not a kid. Don't patronise me."

"Okay. Fine." Gus finished loading his body with guns and turned to Donny, placing a heavy hand on his shoulder. "You want the honest truth?"

"Yes. I think so."

"Right. I have been waiting the last six months, biding my time, looking for the exact right moment to die. To leave all this... shit, behind. And this is it. This is what fate brought to me. Because this is how I go out. This is how I do it."

"You don't mean that."

"Donny, I'm only just starting to like you. Don't make me smack you."

Gus walked back toward the edge of the verge, casting his eyes upon the sea of undead faces. Funny, really. Moments ago, he was full of dread. But standing there, feeling the weight of a dozen guns dragging his body to the floor, gave him a sense of resolution. Like he was home. Like this was where he was meant to be.

"See that sun?" Gus pointed to the sun.

"Yeah," Donny confirmed.

"It's a little down from the middle of the sky,.I make that about two or three in the afternoon. Agree?"

"I guess."

"Well, the girl will be back by the time it's set, and you can't see the sun for the moon no more. Look out for her."

"And you? Where will you be?"

Gus looked at Donny, holding a lingering gaze in the young man's direction.

"Good luck to you," he said, and ran down the slope without looking back.

37

Bill swung the axe around the basement like it was the lead of a rabid dog.

Kristine pushed herself and Laney against the far wall, keeping them out of reach of the wayward weapon. No sooner had Bill decided that it was time they freed themselves of the basement than he had punched through the glass concealing the axe fixed to the wall for the eventuality of a fire and began wielding it with the control of a madman.

"Bill, I really think we should think about this," Katrina urged him.

"What, you reckon we're better off down here, canoodling every night?" Bill narrowed his eyes into a leer that sent a fiery shudder up Kristine's inner thigh. She pushed her hand harder against Laney, unknowingly concealing her from the perverted danger before them.

"No!" Laney objected. "You do not hurt Mrs Andrews anymore!"

Bill grinned wildly. His free hand twitched inside his pocket.

The sick bastard was enjoying her feistiness.

"You've hurt her enough, you won't hurt her anymore!"

"It's okay, Laney, it's okay," Kristine whispered. "It's all right, I'm okay, we're going to be okay."

"How can you lie to her?" Bill asked, that twisted look in his eye he got whenever he wanted to say something provocative for the sake of intensifying her helpless hatred further.

"All I mean," said Kristine, "is that we should come up with a plan. We don't know what's on the other side of that wall."

"A plan?" He let out a large, audible, "Hah!"

"Bill, please."

"How's this for a plan?"

He charged up the stairs, forcing each wooden step to buckle under the pressure of his stubbornness. He twisted the lock open for the first time in God knows how long and placed his hand on the door.

There was no use objecting. No use reasoning with a man that had Bill's sick temperament and odious nature. He was going through that door, and unleashing whatever was on the other side of it upon them.

Kristine had to move. She had to get Laney to that door. If a flood of the infected poured down those stairs, they would be trapped. They had the best chance of survival if they pounded up those stairs and embraced the inevitable chaos.

She crouched beside Laney, looked her in the eyes with the best comforting expression she could muster, and held her hands solidly and reassuringly on her dainty biceps.

"Laney, listen to me. We've got to go through that door. Whatever happens, take hold of my hand, and do not let go. You understand?"

Laney gave an eager nod.

"I trust you, Mrs Andrews."

What a line.

What a terrible, loving line.

She trusts me.

That was the worst thing the poor girl could have said.

It meant that whatever happened to that girl was on Kristine. It would be her responsibility, and her burden to bear.

The sound of the door swinging open and bashing against the inner wall was met with a set of eager groans from the other side. Bill's defiant scream rang out, and the lights of the corridor flickered as he disappeared from the corner of Kristine's vision.

She grabbed hold of Laney's hand and took her as quickly as she could up the stairs and to the doorway. As soon as she reached it she halted, and looked at what they were dealing with.

To her right, Bill was swinging the axe to and fro, waving it about. He smacked it into the head of decaying faces whose eyes still sprung open, slicing it through the chests of running corpses with their innards tumbling out.

Whatever she thought of him, he was giving it a good go.

But there were so many of them. And their numbers were growing thicker.

With every thrust Bill let out a scream. This only seemed to attract the attention of more dormant bodies down the far side of the long stretch of corridor.

She urged him to stop.

She said nothing, but she wished it with all her might.

But he didn't.

He never did stop when she wanted.

She looked to her left. More infected were coming at them from the distance, emerging from all the classrooms down the corridor.

Where had Bill said that the media studies room was? The one with the radio?

Two doors down.

She saw it. Two doors to her left. A door with the sign *Media Studies* fixed upon it. They could make it. She was positive they could make it.

"Come on!" she urged Laney.

She took the girl's hand and dragged her, ducking the outstretched arms of an approaching walking corpse clambering reaching for her.

They made it inside just in time for her to swing the door closed in the face of a running beast, whose forehead smacked into the door, forcing blood and a rogue eye to slide down the square of glass at the top of the door.

She twisted the lock, then backed away.

Bill's face abruptly peered in the door's small window. He looked alert. The initial confidence he had upon launching his attack was gone. All around him were faces of the undead, descending upon him, clawing at him.

"Let me in!" Bill screamed.

Kristine didn't move.

She gripped Laney's hand to make sure she didn't do anything either.

"Let me in! Let me in, you fucking bitch!"

Kristine dragged Laney to the far corner and jumped at the sight of a dead body. Unlike the others, this one lay still, and without a face. In its hands was a shotgun pointed toward his absent chin, held by a hand that was home to a clear, red bite mark. Over the wall behind him, pieces of his brain had crusted to the wall.

She turned and gagged, doing her best not to be sick.

Laney stared at it, but did nothing. Said nothing.

Kristine turned her away and shielded her.

Kristine looked to the door. Bill was gone.

"Wait here," she instructed Laney.

Kristine ran to the window, which was on the opposite side of the room to the door. It was smashed, but a few floors up and out of reach of any zombie below. Her eyes squinted from the light of the harsh sun, taking a while to readjust; she had almost forgotten what it looked like. The wind was light and refreshing on her face, but with the subtle breeze came the stench of rotting meat. She looked below her and noticed the car park was full of the infected, helplessly roaming about. None of them running, thinking, doing anything but limping aimlessly.

She gasped and flung herself backwards, out of sight, and out of smell – she wasn't completely sure what would attract their attention, but she did not want to take any risks.

Unbeknownst to her, as all of this had happened, Laney had wandered across the room, her eyes fixed on the small piece of glass in the door.

Kristine turned around and immediately grabbed onto her.

"Laney, what are you doing?!"

It was too late.

Bill's face smacked against the glass.

But it wasn't Bill.

It was his face, his body, his disgusting, lecherous features – but whatever soul he had was gone. His eyes were yellow, his face ripped apart. He was one of them.

Laney screamed. An ear-piercing, shredding scream that went right through Kristine.

She quickly covered Laney's mouth with her hand.

But it was too late.

Once Laney had stopped, the sounds from the school's exterior grew bigger. The moans and groans outside the smashed window were no longer aimless wandering of helpless figures – they were determined growls. Hungry assailants, gathering for fresh blood.

She edged toward the window and peered out.

They barged against the wall of the school, all of them amassing into a riot. There was not a space free of them. They had descended upon the car park in an instant, and more were galloping toward them, their ravenous eyes searching for their dinner. As far as she could see, their faces went on, chattering their loose teeth and smacking their cracked lips. They were clearly starving; their dead skin drooped from their bones, their mouths opening and closing like a fish in a bowl waiting to be fed.

And they were trapped.

From outside in the corridor.

From outside of the school.

The radio. It was their only chance. Across the room, next to the only corpse that didn't move – it was there.

Just as she noticed it, the door to the room began to buckle.

38

As Gus reached the base of the hill, it truly dawned on him that he had no idea what he was doing.

There were thousands of them. Tens of thousands. More, even.

He'd fought against the odds before, but this was something else.

He had his machine gun over his back, Uzis on his belt, blade by his ankle, ammo over his shoulder, guns by his side – but he had never felt more naked.

What was he supposed to do? The place would be blown to pieces in hours, and he was somehow supposed to locate the girl, extract her, and be back in time to watch as if they were having a firework display.

His best plans occurred when he winged it. But even so...

Just as doubt had begun to succeed in clouding his mind, the sound of the zombies grew less. Their groans began to move, their smell becoming less potent, and before Gus knew it, the ground was shaking with the tremble of thousands of feet thudding against it.

He backed up the hill to get a better view. His mouth hung open in disbelief.

There was a stampede of the undead pounding away, into the distance. The backs of their heads disappeared from view within seconds, all aimed in the same direction.

Before Gus could make sense of it, the mass of bodies pressing against the sturdy walls had turned to a barren, empty car park, with pieces of litter floating in the breeze.

This must be the luckiest moment he ever had in his life.

Yet there was something about this...

It was too easy.

And as the reasoning of the action of the infected occurred to him, his perception on what had happened faded from glee at his good luck to the cynical, realistic mind he had become so acquainted with.

There was only one thing that could have attracted that horde of starving zombies that had been deprived of meat for so long, to sprint in the same definite direction.

Living flesh.

The girl. It must be her. She must have attracted the attention of one infected, then the rest of them followed...

It meant she was alive.

Though possibly not for long.

Well, at least I know which way to go...

Without another moment's hesitation, he seized his opportunity. He leapt upon the wiry fence, dragging his body upwards and perching upon the top. He pushed his body out in an almighty leap and landed succinctly atop the stone wall that had separated him from the hungry corpses' dryly salivating mouths.

He looked back with a fleeting glance at the concerned faces of Donny and Sadie.

They must be thinking the same thing. They must have a good guess why all the undead ran in the same direction.

He lowered himself down, hanging from the top brick, then let go, being sure to bend his knees to steady his impact, and wincing at the inevitable pain in his calf.

He covered his mouth as dust travelled along the wind. He couldn't let himself cough. He had to be silent. If such a faint, faraway sound as a little girl could attract them so eagerly, the patter of his footsteps or a gentle cough could be just as deadly.

But he was in.

After all the travelling, debating, worrying – he was in.

He retracted the blade from his ankle, gripping it affirmatively. He stayed low as he bolted across the car park to the nearest building, constantly rotating his head, purposefully searching, frequently peering in every direction. Listening to every sound, noticing any change in the wind, and any increase in the potent smell of rotting meat that hung in the air of London.

Pressing himself against the wall of the building, he concluded that he needed to get somewhere high, somewhere he could get a vantage point. The zombies had dictated his direction, but he could easily end up running into the tail end of them, and that would do no good to Laney's chances, or his own mortality.

Sticking against the wall he edged to his right, coming to the corner of the building. As he peered around the corner, he looked upon the grand sign planted upon it. Letters were missing from the business name, but from the look of a foyer and film posters that still hung loosely, he deduced that it was once a cinema. The windows were smashed, and the inside of the building looked black and charred. Faded grey still wandered from the building, evidence of smoke that had dissipated long ago but still clung to the furniture of the building like a possessive ghost.

This was good enough.

He rushed to an empty window frame and stepped over it, carefully avoiding the jagged edges of the glass that still remained in the corners.

Inside the foyer, a zombie lay on the floor. Its arms reached for Gus, but its legs were missing, and its insides hung out of its bottom half.

Gus plunged his knife into its head. He used as much strength as he could, but found that the zombie's skull had turned to delicate crust, and didn't take much coercing.

He ran toward the staircase, taking them two at a time, until he finally reached the roof. He opened the door just as cautiously, surveying every edge and every corner until he concluded it was safe.

As soon as he looked into the distance, he could see where the zombies had taken aim for.

A school.

They surrounded the entire circumference of the building. Even from this distance, he could hear their moans of hunger, their desperation for human flesh. So many of them, scrambling for food.

That was where he needed to go.

I'm coming for you, Laney.

39

Bill's greasy face had never looked so greasy. Every vile aspect of his features had been accentuated, culminating in his yellow pupils intensifying his glare through the thin pane of glass.

Kristine's hand gripped Laney's shoulder. Not that she needed to – Laney was rooted to the spot, barely moving, her eyes fixed on the face of the man who had consistently tormented both of them for the last few months.

Kristine needed to act. She needed to act, or neither of them were going to survive at all.

The radio. That was what they had gone there for, and they needed to use it.

Kristine knelt before Laney. As she placed her hands on her arms, she noticed a damp patch on the inside of her trousers.

"Laney, listen to me," Kristine began. "We need–"

Before Kristine could finish her sentence, there was a loud smash that made her instinctively twist toward the door.

The square of glass had smashed through, and Bill's arm now hung through it, reaching and grabbing at the empty air.

The door pounded against its hinges, buckling

under the pressure of a corridor of bodies.

As Kristine stared, the unequivocal truth dawned on her like a splash of frozen water in the face.

The door's going to break down.

She rushed toward it, pushing her arms against the resistance. She had no idea what she was doing. She in no way had the strength to hold it, but she had to act. She had to.

It was the only way to save Laney.

A large filing cabinet was propped against the adjacent wall. After rushing to its opposite side, she pushed against it with all her might. Her feet skidded against the floor, battling against the weight of loads of heavy paper, but it shifted slightly from her pressure.

A crack spread through the door beneath Bill's reaching arm.

Kristine pushed and pushed, making a little progress, but little was better than none.

Her eyes passed Laney's. They were still there. Staring. Innocent. Terrified.

"Laney, I need you to do something very important for me, can you do that?"

Laney didn't react. She just stared.

Kristine hoped that there was still something beneath that expression of terror, that her catatonic state was not permanent.

"There is a radio on the other side of the room, can you see it? Can you look for me?"

Laney's eyes blinked. She slowly turned to look over her shoulder.

"That's it, keep looking, it's right over there. Do you see it, Laney? Do you?"

Laney gently nodded.

"Good. You're such a good girl, so clever."

Kristine pushed against the filing cabinet. Almost there.

"I need you to go switch it on for me. By the plug, then that black button next to it. Can you do that for me? Can you?"

Laney stared at the radio, her legs glued in place.

"Laney, I need you to go to the radio. I need you to do that now, please."

Laney ran forward, wobbling a little and losing her balance. She pushed herself up – she was always so resilient, such a strong little girl – and she propelled herself at the radio.

Kristine turned her attention back to the filing cabinet. She reached the door, but the cabinet wouldn't go against it. Bill's arm was still there, blocking the cabinet from pressing firmly, stopping her from being able to put up another line of defence.

"Go away!" she cried. "Go away, you horrible, lousy man!"

She took a few steps back, prepared a run-up, then charged herself forward, picking up speed, and jumped hard against the filing cabinet. Her whole shoulder seized in pain, but the cabinet was now against the door. On the floor beside it she could see Bill's decapitated arm, blood spilling like a spilt glass of milk.

She leant against the wall, closing her eyes, breathing, breathing so fast she almost lost the ability. She willed her panting to subside, to calm, but she could just not stop hyperventilating.

"I did it," came the lonely, innocent voice of a young girl.

Kristine turned to Laney, holding a radio to the side. From the speakers beside her came static.

Kristine's heart beat faster. She smiled. It was working. It was actually working.

"Speak into it for me. See what they say."

"Hello," Laney tried. "Hello, is anyone there?"

Kristine smiled widely, so happy, so proud of her.

Within seconds the cabinet collapsed, and five thick fingers had wrapped themselves around Kristine's throat.

There were screams. Kristine couldn't tell whether they came from her or Laney, but they echoed in her mind, reverberating around the emptiness of her consciousness.

She stared into the eyes of Laney as she felt a set of teeth sink into her cheek bone.

40

A blackened plastic bag scurried past Gus's foot, carrying along the wind to join the other strays. The sun was hovering low in the sky, and a dark-orange sunset was close. The beauty of nature above was in stark contrast to the dusty crunch of the earth beneath his feet.

Staying low. Staying hidden. Staying quiet.

Those were the three things Gus kept reminding himself.

The closer he got, the more likely he would be to attract the attention of the horde. A single cough or step on a twig could cost him not only his life, but the freedom to be free from an agonising death. The school was close, which meant that so were they.

As he darted across another car park, he thought he saw a flicker of movement in the distance. He rushed behind an abandoned police car, taking cover.

He listened.

A rustle from the distance indicated the heavy steps of something walking. A few more rustles told Gus that there were a few of them. As he listened – *really* listened – he could hear the rest of them. The horde of thousands, groaning and yapping.

He slithered onto the passenger seat of the police

car. Lifting his head up slowly, spotting the figures illuminated by the horizon, he brought the passenger door slowly to a close and shut it.

A sudden burst of static from the police radio made his body rigid with tension. He ducked down, ducking out of sight, and turned the volume downwards.

He waited.

For a sound. A smell. Something that showed that his location had been blown.

Nothing.

He lifted the radio to his mouth and spoke clearly. "Hello, is anybody there?"

Nothing.

"Hello, is anybody out there?"

Static.

"Can you hear me? Can you–"

Then he thought of something.

The chip. The one Donny was showing off about. Gus had snatched it off Donny in irritation. And he had put it…

He reached into his inside pocket and pulled it out.

"Donny, you beauty!" he declared, then felt glad Donny hadn't been around to hear it.

He opened the back of the radio, placed the chip in, then turned it back around.

Sure enough, it went through every possible frequency. Every lapse in static, every faint whisper, until it landed on one station.

He could hear something.

Something faint. A voice. A girl's voice.

He slowly twisted the volume knob to the side, bringing the volume gently up so that he could only just hear it.

"Hello?"

He twisted the volume up again, only enough so that the voice became clear.

"Hello, is anyone there?"

The voice was shaking, a constant tremble under its fevered desperation. A young girl. Terrified. Despairing.

It must be her. It must be.

The gentle buzz of static abruptly pounded through the speakers as it mixed with a violent scream. Gus's hand clamped around the volume control, turning it right back down again.

The screaming didn't stop.

She didn't stop.

Gus picked up his side of the radio and pressed it against his mouth.

"I'm receiving you, are you still there?"

More screaming.

Just more manic, ear-piercing screaming.

"I'm receiving, come in?"

He flinched. It was so high-pitched that it went through his entire body.

"Laney?"

The scream ceased.

"Laney, is that you?"

Static.

In the background there were groans, distant shouts, someone suffering incredulous pain.

"Laney, please answer me."

"How do you know my name?" came a timid, inquisitive voice.

"Laney, listen to me, I've been sent to save you."

Nothing. Just distant chaos.

"Laney, can you hear me?"

"Yes."

"Laney, I'm here to help, just – just tell me what is happening."

"My teacher – she…"

"She what, Laney? What happened?"

"He's hurting her. He's… eating…"

Gus wiped a bead of sweat from his bow.

As he did, an idea came to mind.

It wasn't a great one – but it was an idea. And it would have to do.

"Laney, I'm here to save you, okay. Do you understand?"

"Yes."

"Do you believe me?"

"What?"

"That I'm here to save you, do you believe me?"

"Yes. They are–"

Another scream.

"Laney, I need you to listen to me, I need you to not scream. It will only attract more of them. I know it's tough, but you just need to not scream."

"… Okay."

"Good. Well done. You're being so strong. Now, is there a window in the room you're in? A window you can safely get to?"

"Yes."

"Good. Now get to that window and tell me what you see."

A moment of silence.

The sun began sinking into the distance, and a grey darkness grew stronger.

"There are lots of them, there are – there are so

many of them! They are all looking at me!"

"Laney, can you see the entrance to the school? I mean, if you look, can you see it?"

"They are at the entrance."

"Is the entrance to your left, or your right?"

"It's... My left."

"And how many windows are there between you and it?"

"Er... Three, I think."

Gus made a decision.

Possibly a bad one, but the only one he had.

"Well done, Laney, you're being so strong, you're being such a good girl. Now listen to me very carefully. I'm going to tell you what I need you to do. Are you listening, Laney?"

"Yes."

The manoeuvre. The handbrake turn. The twisting of the car he had failed to get correct twice in the past two days.

It was the only way.

The only chance he had.

"When I tell you, and only when I tell you, I need you to do this for me. And I need you to trust me."

I can do this. I have to do this.

"Okay."

God, I hope I can do this.

"Laney, I need you to jump out of the window."

41

"What?" yelped Laney, her eyes glued to her teacher slumped on the floor, her eyes wide and empty.

The crack in the door had grown bigger, and arms were now reaching through it.

Mrs Andrews's hand twitched.

How was it twitching?

Half of the skin on her face was gone, leaving a bloody mess. Her throat was an open, gaping wound. Yet her fingers were still twitching.

Maybe she was alive? Maybe she was okay?

"Did   you   hear   me,   Laney?"

"I – I –"

"I know it sounds crazy, but you need to take a leap of faith, and you need to trust me. Can you do that?"

She turned back to the window, looking down at the faces looking back up at her. They were all so pale. And skin was missing, just like Mrs Andrews. And their eyes, they were empty. So empty. They all looked angry, all like they wanted to hurt her, she couldn't jump into them, she couldn't.

"I can't jump!"

"I know, Laney, I know how it sounds. But I'm going to save you. This is how I'm going to save you."

"No."

It was so far down. And there were so many of them. Their hands reaching up for her, clutching like the way Bill's hands used to clutch at Mrs Andrews. Did they want to hurt her like Bill had hurt Mrs Andrews?

And there were so many… So many of them… So many, she couldn't see the end.

A groan. It came from inside the room. From behind her.

Mrs Andrew's whole hand was twitching. Both of them. And her arms. Except, they weren't moving like they should. It was a disjointed twitch, like her bones weren't connected. There was something wrong with it. Laney couldn't figure out what it was, but there was something wrong.

"Laney, the only way to save you is for you to jump. Get ready, I'm almost there."

Mrs Andrews's legs suddenly shifted position. And again. And again. Each time twisting a different way.

"Okay," Laney agreed. "Okay, I'll do it."

Sirens in the distance. Somewhere behind the hum of all those hungry groans, was a police siren.

Was this man a policeman? Maybe that's why he was trying to help her.

Mrs Andrews's eyes shot open.

"My teacher is awake!"

"Laney, has she been bitten? Tell me if she's been bitten?"

"She… She's been hurt."

"Okay, Laney, just stay by the window, stay calm, I am almost there."

The sirens grew louder. The roar of an engine screeched closer. A mass of thuds, like lots of solid objects hitting other solid objects with full force. It was getting louder than the groans.

Mrs Andrews pushed herself to her feet. Her eyes stayed on Laney the whole time, a low murmur like a croaky cough vibrating from her throat.

She stumbled forward.

"Okay, Laney, I want you to jump, in five."

Blood dribbled down Mrs Andrews's chin, trickling onto the floor, forming a puddle.

Her joints stiffened. Her bones reformed. They all clicked into place.

The sound of thuds against metal grew closer.

"Four."

The sirens were deafening now.

The thuds were repetitive, constant, pow, pow, smack, bump, all the time, again and again.

"Three."

Mrs Andrews snarled.

Except, this wasn't Mrs Andrews.

Laney could see that.

"Two."

The corpse charged forward with a high-pitched screech, sprinting toward Laney.

She screamed.

"One."

She held her breath like she was diving underwater and leapt over the side of the window pane. Mrs Andrews followed behind and went tumbling to the ground.

Before she hit the floor, a car screeched into position beneath her. With the sound of a handbrake skidding harshly, the car twisted in a perfectly formed circle. The door opened, and a man stuck out of it, a large man with his arm outstretched. As if by perfectly timed magic, she fell into the man's arms and was thrown into the backseat before she could tell what was going on.

The thudding started again. It was louder now. So, so loud. The sirens wailed, but the constant smacks repeated.

She leant up and peered over the man's shoulder. His windscreen wipers were going so fast, wiping red gunk off his screen at a rapid pace. The car was speeding with such force that she felt they would crash at any moment, but they didn't, they just kept pounding into the zombies before them.

And the man was screaming. He was in a lot of pain. Holding onto his calf.

"Son of a bitch," he grunted. "Motherfucker!" he screamed.

Then his grimace changed. Amongst the pain, he looked to be laughing. A strange, uncontrollable laugh of triumph. Like he had just achieved something that was impossible.

It looked as if the pain had gone and elation had taken over.

"I can't believe it," the man was saying. "I did it. I did it. I really fucking did it! And all I had to do was withstand a *lot* of bloody pain!"

The man turned over his shoulder and looked at Laney.

"Hi," he said. "How are you?"

Laney's jaw hung open with stuttering sounds drifting out.

"My name is Gus Harvey," he continued. "It's nice to meet you."

She looked at his speedometer. He was going over a hundred miles per hour. Bashing zombies out the way with such frequency there was no way he could see where he was going. Even though she knew she couldn't, she felt like she was able to feel the aerodynamic force pushing through her hair.

"Thank you for saving me," was all she could muster.

And it was enough.

For Gus, it was always enough.

Minus One Hour Twenty Minutes

Rick Wood

42

Donny shifted his weight from right foot to left. His shoulders tensed upwards as he nervously strummed one hand through the other.

Darkness had fully descended. The sun had disappeared, and the moon was now rising into the sky.

He remembered Gus's hollow words.

The girl will be back by the time it's set, and you can't see the sun for the moon no more.

Donny hadn't seen the sun in a while. The moon had been a sturdy presence, filling the sky with a gentle illumination.

He peered into the empty streets of London before him.

He turned to Sadie, who sat on the floor, uprooting flowers, inquisitively running her eyes over them, then throwing them to the side.

"Sadie," Donny spoke, crouching before her. "I – I'm going in."

Sadie's eyebrows narrowed to a glare.

"I know it sounds crazy," Donny persisted, "but I have to. Gus said he'd be back by now, and he–"

Donny stopped talking. Looked into Sadie's eyes. He thought she was glaring at him, but in actual fact, her eyes were fixed on something over Donny's shoulder.

"What is it? Is it zombies?"

Sadie rose to her feet and lurched her body forward, hissing at something.

Donny looked behind him. He saw nothing.

"Sadie, I don't see anything."

She hissed again. But just as her eyes intensified and she readied her body to run, something struck her around the back of her head, forcing her limp body to fall to the floor.

Donny looked at the assailant.

He couldn't believe his eyes.

It wasn't possible. It was not possible. There was no way. Absolutely no way. It must be a lie. A mirage. Something.

It couldn't be.

"But... I shot you."

"Yes, sir, you did," Stacey answered, with a beaming smile and a sparkle in her eyes.

"I shot you in the chest. Three times."

"Yes, you did – and it rather hurt, quite a bit actually. *I* didn't think it was very nice."

Weapons. Donny needed weapons.

They were in the boot of the car.

Just a few steps away.

He edged to his left. Toward the boot. Nice and slow. So she wouldn't pounce, wouldn't do anything. Just slowly, getting minutely closer to the boot full of weapons.

"I don't understand. How are you not dead?"

Stacey lifted up her spotty dress, revealing the undeveloped body of a ten-year-old girl, except it was covered in wounds. There were three definite holes from the shots Donny had fired, gaping open and crusted with dried blood. Below those were knife wounds, and another circular scar – possibly a bullet wound that had healed long ago.

And on her leg. The most pertinent scar of all.

A bite wound.

"How are you alive?" Donny asked.

"Oh, you mean the zombie bite? Yeah, I was bitten."

"But – you're not dead."

"No, silly, of course I'm not. I mean, do I look like I'm dead?"

"I don't understand."

Keep her talking. Edge toward the car. Keep her talking.

The weapons in the boot.

Just keep her talking.

"You need to shoot a zombie in the head, everybody knows that. Which is why you managed to hurt Daddy – which, by the way, was not nice."

"You don't look like a zombie."

He was a few steps from the bonnet. He was nearly there.

"My family has special genes."

Realisation hit Donny like a sucker punch to the gut.

She was immune to the virus.

How was that even possible?

"See, I have those special genes. Daddy had those special genes. Mommy has those special genes. And my sister."

Her sister?

Stacey looked to the unconscious body of Sadie lying on the floor.

What the fuck...

Donny was close enough now.

He turned and ran, keeping his eyes on Stacey, reaching for the boot.

He tripped over a foot and went flying to the floor, landing on his face. He lifted himself to his knees, wiping a trickle of blood from his nose.

"I suppose you thought you were being rather sneaky."

Trisha sat on the floor, leant against the boot, cradling Gus's shotgun like a baby in her arms.

"Jolly nice weapons, though. Really, I admire them. James would have loved them."

Donny closed his eyes.

He didn't want to be eaten. He barely wanted to be killed, never mind eaten.

He was screwed. Completely and utterly screwed.

Gus, this would be a really good time for you to come back.

But Gus wasn't coming back.

He said he'd be back by now. And he wasn't.

Which could surely mean only one thing.

He turned and looked to Trisha's face. Her smile curved upwards. One could mistake her for being cheerful, except for her eyes. They gave her away. It was the same look in Gus's eyes. That same faraway absence that no one could touch.

The look of someone who had lost their family.

Donny took to his feet and ran. It was the only thing he could do.

A loud shot rang out and Donny felt a warm pain pummel through the back of his ankle. He collapsed onto the floor, writhing in agony.

"Now, I really did not want to have to do that," Trisha declared, standing over him. "Any time I shoot you, I am losing good meat."

Donny looked up at her, toughening his expression, refusing to let her know that the scraping of the passing bullet was causing his leg to seize in agony.

"And you know, I do not like to waste meat."

It dawned on Donny what they had done with her husband's corpse.

Stacey joined her mother, giving her a big, loving, bear hug.

"I'm hungry," she said.

"That's okay, darling. It's dinner time now."

Minus One Hour

Rick Wood

43

How the fuck can something so dead run so fast?

Gus's foot pressed hard on the accelerator, forcing the car forward and screeching around every corner. The smell of burning rubber followed him, the speed dial steadily hovering somewhere between fifty and eighty.

Yet, in his windscreen mirror, he could see the horde, still sprinting after him. Even in the car he could feel the ground shaking, rumbling under the weight of so many heavy feet.

"How you doin', Laney?" Gus asked.

If felt so strange to say that name again. Especially to a girl so young. So vulnerable. So helpless.

Just like she was when she died.

Stop it.

Must focus.

"They are still coming!" she yelped, staring out of the back window.

"Then stop looking. It's like when you're really high up, you know? Best advice is – just don't look down."

"Who are you?" she asked.

"Me? I'm…"

Good question.

Who was he?

He wasn't in the army. He wasn't a secret agent. He was just some alcoholic nutcase that they saw as expendable enough to send on a suicide mission.

"I'm... nobody. Just a guy. Sent to rescue a girl."

Well that sounded cliché.

Still, it was good enough for her, and she seemed to relax – but only for a moment, then she turned back to the window and resumed her terrified stare.

Gus hit the brakes, then swung around another corner.

The cinema grew closer.

They were nearly there.

"Hold on!"

He fired them into the car park, ignoring the eager groans and frantic moans chasing behind them.

He brought the car to a stop beside the stone wall that separated London from the rest of the country. As soon he had skidded to a halt, he burst out of the car and opened the backdoor. He grabbed Laney and climbed on top of the car.

"Listen to me," he told her. "I'm going to swing you over the wall, do you understand?"

"What?" Her eyebrows raised, her lip trembled, her body shook.

"We don't have time to think about it – I'm going to swing you and throw you over that wall. Then there is a man and a girl waiting by a car. You go to them, you understand? They will take you home."

"But–"

Before she could object, he grabbed her hands and began swinging. Spinning a few times, getting enough force, ignoring her continuous scream, and let go as he directed her upwards. She flew over the wall, disappearing behind it.

She was safe.

He'd done it.

He stayed atop the police car.

The horde thudded into the far side of the car park.

All of them, parading forward, their arms outstretched for him.

They were seconds away.

He took the pills from his pocket.

It was time.

He was going to be reunited with his family.

The horde were halfway across the car park. A thousand old friends joining him for lunch.

He put the pills in his mouth.

44

Janet's sweet smile reached out for Gus.

Those eyes. Those damn perfect eyes. Glazing over with tears.

Bitten.

Those eyes turning yellow. Turning to terror. Becoming something Gus had never seen before.

How he longed to kiss her. To touch her face, to run his hand down her gentle skin. To hold her close during a thunderstorm. To hold her hand as she gave birth. To kiss her on their wedding day.

Love like theirs only existed in movies. It wasn't just a standard marriage, where you exist together. It was earth-shattering. World-changing. After so many years, she still made his heart race. He would still wake up in the morning, looking at her sleeping peacefully beside him, and wonder how he got so damn lucky.

Men like him didn't get things like this.

Then his daughter would run in. Her eyes would light up the room stronger than the early morning sun. For the entirety of their Sunday morning they would lay in bed together, laughing, playing. Being the family that you only saw in catalogues. The family that everyone else envied.

He would kiss his wife on her forehead. Ruffle his

daughter's hair.

And he would tell them he loved them.

Every morning he would tell them he loved them.

Janet would not want him to be living like this.

Neither of them would.

Gus opened his eyes.

The horde reached the base of the police car he stood upon. Reached out for him. Clambered at his feet.

But he knew it's not what they would have wanted.

Janet would not want them to be reunited. Not yet. Not until the time was right. When it was nature's choice, not his.

She would kill to see his face again.

But not like this.

He spat out the pills.

Turned to the wall.

It was too big.

A hand grabbed his ankle and he shook it off.

The car was beginning to rock. Nudging from side to side. Keeping his balance was becoming tough, as was staying out of the reach of the all the zombies clambering for him.

He jumped, trying for the top of the wall.

He just needed another metre.

He looked to the pale, demented faces below, chopping their jaws at him. He had an idea.

He placed his feet shoulder width apart and rocked the car back and forth. Using the momentum that the zombies had created, he forced it further into an uneasy rock.

The car swung upwards and landed onto its side.

Seizing the opportunity, Gus jumped onto the side

of the upturned car.

Just as the car turned once again beneath his feet, he used it to gain the extra metre he needed and jumped upwards, reaching his hands out for the top of the wall. One hand scraped off, but the other held tight.

His fingers slipped.

They were reaching for him.

He swung his other hand up, attempting to hold on more securely.

His entire body weight was being held by the strength of a few fingers.

He slipped again, but held on. He pushed his arm upwards, until he had securely mounted the top of the wall.

Using his feet as leverage, he pushed his body up, ignoring the continual pain of his calf, and rolled onto the top of the wall.

He lay there for a few moments, allowing his breathing to calm, finally feeling himself overcome with exhaustion. He had denied himself rest for so long that now he was able to lay on something flat, he could feel each ache in every muscle.

Pushing himself to his feet, he leapt to the wire fence and climbed down. He pushed himself up the verge of the hill, making it to the car, where Laney stood beside Sadie.

He smiled at the sight of them.

Now it was just the drive back. That was it. It was over, and all he had to do was drive. He had achieved the impossible.

He walked to the door of the car, placed his hand on the handle, then stopped.

Something wasn't right.

He looked to Sadie, who stood still, staring at him with wounded eyes.

Something was going on.

He looked around himself.

"Where's Donny?" he asked.

Sadie looked blankly back at him.

"Where is he?"

Sadie looked down.

"People," she said. "Took him. Away."

Gus closed his eyes and bowed his head. Why? Why did that inept kid have to do this?

He looked to Laney, looking back at him with those big, innocent eyes.

The mission was the most important thing.

He couldn't go back. He couldn't wait any longer. London was going up in flames, he hadn't enough time. He had one purpose, one sole purpose, and that was the girl.

Laney.

He had to get her back to her father.

If only someone had thought that about his girl.

"Get in the car," he demanded, placing Laney in the passenger seat.

"Donny!" Sadie protested, furiously shaking her head.

"Get in the car, or I'll soddin' leave you too!"

Gus sat in the driver's seat, waiting for Sadie to reluctantly get in. Once she did, he paused.

Then he drove away, watching London grow smaller in the rear-view mirror.

Rick Wood

Minus Forty Minutes

Rick Wood

45

Gus ran his fingers through his thick hair.

The motorway was clear, and the drive home seemed to be taking far less time than the forward journey had.

A glance in the mirror showed him that Sadie was still sulking. Her arms folded, her eyebrows pushed downwards, and her irritated eyes focussed on him in the mirror.

"I told you," Gus said. "We can't go back."

Sadie's expression did not falter.

Gus glanced at Laney in the passenger seat next to him, soundly asleep.

"We had a mission. It was to extract the target. We have done that. We can't go back for a fallen soldier."

He thought about all the times it had been true. In Afghanistan, when they had to clear the area and leave a fallen comrade behind.

But he'd have wanted them to do the same.

The mission is the most important thing. Above all else, the mission is important. As is brotherhood and loyalty to your fellow soldiers, yes – but if the squad returned for that soldier they left behind, it would be more than one dead.

Still, Sadie's expression remained the same.

"We don't even know if he's still alive. And besides, you are important, too."

She was.

She had survived a zombie bite. Her blood had mixed with that of the infected, and she was alive. Not properly, but she was alive. She could be the solution to this mess.

He hesitated. Looked out the window at the burnt-out cars and corpses with exploded heads. The destruction of the world. A world that, until a few days ago, Gus couldn't see being saved.

"Your blood, Sadie, may have the key to... I don't know. I don't know science, I don't know how it works, but ultimately, you're a zombie without the... zombieness. You are important. More so than me, or Donny, or..."

No.

She was never going to understand.

She was a child. Barely even that. She was an animal. She had the disposition of a feral human being. She had no cognition, no ability to talk. She relied on instinct. She was, ultimately, one of them – only she didn't try and kill people.

Instead, she saved them.

And she had saved them. Protected them from an oncoming horde. Done it all single-handedly.

He sighed.

He looked to Laney.

Something glistened by her feet. Something reflecting the full moon. Something...

Donny's sunglasses.

The little weirdo, going on about his sunglasses.

But he was so chuffed with them. He wore them,

and would not stop smiling, and…

And he went after Gus. When he could have left. He went after Gus and forced himself to shoot someone. Something that took so much out of him.

Donny had barely been able to lift a gun.

Yet Donny had pointed that gun, fooled the man into thinking he wouldn't, then pulled the trigger.

He had saved Gus's life.

But the mission.

The mission was most important.

No one would understand how important.

But why? A politician's daughter's life was not more precious than anyone else's.

God damn, this is tough.

He looked back in his mirror. Sadie's glare still focussed on him. That intense stare, those fixed eyes.

She was mouthing something.

Whispering something.

Gus strained to hear what it was.

And he heard, ever so slightly:

"Friend."

Gus brought the car to a sudden halt.

He let out a large, aggressive growl. Furious with himself. Loathing his weak temperament for what he was about to do.

He spun the car in a circle and turned back, speeding as fast as the car would take him.

46

Heat radiated against Donny's flesh, illuminating him with a flickering amber glow. He coughed as his lungs rejected the mouthfuls of smoke he was forced to keep swallowing. As his eyes readjusted, orange blurs transformed to the terrifying sight of the flames that were going to cook his flesh.

As soon as he realised what the fire was for, a pertinent thought hit the forefront of his mind.

Why am I alive?

He went to move his hands. He couldn't. Something was stopping him, something that was burning his wrists. Rope.

He tried his feet. His ankles too were burning from the rubbing of harsh, bristly rope.

A draught floated against his back, and it abruptly occurred to him that he was half-clothed.

"Help!" he immediately shouted. "Help! Please!"

"Aw, are you waking up?" came the patronising voice of a ten-year-old girl behind him. "You really are infantile, aren't you?"

"What?"

Stacey flopped to the floor beside Donny and began drawing things in the soil with her finger.

"If you shout out, all you'll do is attract zombies,

and they will eat you far sooner than we will."

"You – you – you psycho bitch!"

Stacey gasped and slapped him hard across the face.

"Mummy says you are not supposed to use language like that! It is not becoming of a gentleman, or a lady."

His eyes switched between the fire and Stacey. To the fire. To Stacey.

Why am I still alive?

"Listen, please, just let me go," Donny begged. "You don't need to do this. There is still plenty of food available. You can do it other ways."

"You mean canned goods?" came Trisha's voice as she walked past with her arms full of logs that she dumped on the ever-growing fire. "How ghastly! Really, why settle for such things when you can eat like queens?"

"But I am a human, it is wrong!"

"How so? You eat chicken, do you not? Pig? Cow? You think they die by magic? No, they tie them up and slit their throats. You're no different."

These people were crazy. Mental. A bizarre mixture of etiquette and sociopathy. Is this what the zombie apocalypse had done to them?

Maybe not.

Maybe they had been doing this for a while, and the sour events of the world had just freed them of having to do it in private.

"Please, I will give you whatever you want, I'll do whatever, please…"

"Stacey, darling, would you gag him? He is starting to get quite irritating."

"Yes, Mummy."

"No, please, no—"

Stacey took a roll of duct tape, ripped off a piece, and stretched it across Donny's mouth.

He tried begging more. Tried reasoning, but only inaudible sounds were coming out.

"Mummy, can I kill him now? He is *so* annoying."

Why am I still alive? Why have they not killed me yet?

Stacey took a large blade and ran it between her hands.

"Soon, darling, soon. Then I will let you butcher him in whatever way you wish!" Trisha smiled at her daughter as if rewarding her with a special treat, one that was greeted with a huge smile in return.

"Thank you, Mummy."

"You don't want anything rotten stuck in your teeth, do you now, darling?"

"No, Mummy."

That's when it occurred to him.

The answer to his question.

I know why I'm still alive...

Because they were trying to keep him fresh.

47

Gus brought the car to a slow halt on the grassy verge overlooking London. The masses of undead had regathered and were continuing to push against the walls, which seemed to be losing their solidity. From afar they looked to be standing strong, but to Gus's astute, focussed eyes, he could swear he saw the wall buckle.

He turned to Sadie, then looked to Laney still asleep in the seat beside him.

"I need you to stay here," Gus instructed her.

"No! Donny!"

"I know you want to save Donny, but leave that to me. I need you to protect this girl, do you understand?"

Sadie folded her arms and stuck out her bottom lip.

Gus pointed at Laney.

"Friend. See? Friend. Needs your help."

Sadie looked at Laney, then back to Gus. Her arms dropped to her lap and she nodded.

Gus left a despondent smile lingering in the car and made his way to the boot. He took out a machine gun, placed ammo over his shoulder, and made his way to the opening of the woods beside the car.

His eyes scanned the ground, looking for tracks. Footprints. Evidence of feet sliding across the ground.

Finally, he found it. Faint, but definitely there. There were two lines where Donny's feet must have been dragged. Gus could also make out two sets of prints. One that looked like a set of adult's trainers. And one that looked like…

Bare feet.

Child's feet.

No. It couldn't be.

Donny shot her. The little girl was thrown onto her back, and the mother ran for it. How could the little girl be alive? The mother surely wouldn't abandon her otherwise?

But there they were. Child's footprints.

How many children would drag people away?

More pertinently, how could a girl take three shots to the chest and survive?

But then again, six months ago, you could have asked – how would the dead get up and start walking? But they did.

And until a few days ago, you could ask how someone would be immune to a zombie bite.

But there's the answer sitting in the backseat of the car.

He took the safety off the machine gun and edged between the trees, cautiously twisting his head back and forth, looking for signs of the demented family that tried to eat him not too long ago.

The tracks continued to occur steadily through the narrow footpath, then veered off it. Branches, trees, nettles, bushes, all encompassed the new path he would have to forge. The tracks disappeared with the lack of set path, and he would have to rely on observing which trees looked the most disturbed.

He crouched low and moved slowly forward, keeping himself camouflaged by the green that surrounded him.

Rick Wood

Minus Twenty Minutes

Rick Wood

48

A victory cigar hung out the end of Eugene's lips like it was an extension of his tongue.

He tapped the ash out on a lavish, glass ashtray, then took a slow, delightful sip of his seventy-year-old whiskey from his tumbler with decorated carvings around its base.

He huffed. Closed his eyes. Leant back in his chair. Savoured the silence.

Savoured it because it wouldn't be staying for long.

Soon the commotion would begin. His façade would continue. His game face would have to be on.

His intercom buzzed.

He sighed and pressed the button that allowed him to communicate with Sandra, his secretary, taking a moment to ready himself for a long few hours.

"Yes?"

"Prime Minister, General Boris Hayes is here."

"Very good. Just keep him for a moment, I'll tell you when I'm ready."

"Right you are, sir."

He stood. Finished his whiskey. Took a final, long intake of his thick cigar, holding the smoke in his mouth, then released it without a single temptation to cough. He patted the end out in his ashtray, wafted the smoke away, then emptied the ashtray into the bin.

He took a few strides towards the mirror, where he paused.

Looked himself in the eyes.

He was surprised he could look himself in the eyes, but as it turns out, he wasn't easily affected by carrying out genocidal actions. Maybe he was a psychopath. Maybe he wasn't. Or maybe he just faced the reality that people did what they wanted, and needed, for their own sake – and anyone who did not face that reality would be left behind to rot.

Or, in these days, get eaten.

He smoothed down his collar. Straightened up his tie. Fixed his top button.

The intercom buzzed.

"Sir, the general is insisting it's urgent."

Oh, that insufferable wench. Did he not tell her to wait? Was that such a difficult instruction?

She would be getting fired tomorrow.

She'd probably cry. Beg for him to forgive her. Tell him all about her young boy she cares so much about and is just trying to protect and yadda yadda yadda.

These people do go on a bit. If anything, it just makes him more adamant about getting rid of them.

The intercom buzzed once again.

"Sir?"

He let a groan whisper past his lips.

He shuffled his jacket, smoothed down his sleeves, and tightened his cufflinks.

A few slow-paced, smooth steps and he had arrived at the intercom.

"I thought I told you to wait."

"I know, sir, but he's insisting."

"I do not wish to repeat myself."

"…Erm, okay, sir. Sorry."

He swept his hand through his hair, wiping it to the side.

A map of the world was pinned to the wall. He had shaded the five countries that were coming to his aid.

France. Canada. Ukraine. Spain. Japan.

Some of the only places not to fall.

That would change.

He pressed his finger upon the intercom.

"Let him in."

A few seconds later, General Boris Hayes strode hastily into the room, clutching a radio to his face.

"Hello, Boris."

"Prime Minister, our allies are airborne. They are waiting for confirmation."

Eugene looked at his watch. Seeing as he hadn't heard from Gus Harvey and that irritable man Donny Jevon for a few days, he assumed they had perished.

Shame; he thought they'd last longer.

Well. At least it looked like he had made the effort. That had been Gus Harvey's purpose, and it would be on record for when the time came.

"How long do we have, Boris?"

"An hour from when you give the word."

Eugene nodded. He turned toward Boris, looking him in the eye. A seasoned veteran. A decorated war hero. Someone so wise, so experienced, yet ready to walk right into his demise.

"Okay, General. Give the order."

"Roger, sir." Boris squeezed the trigger on his radio. "Confirmation received."

"Affirmative," came the response on the radio.

Boris looked to Eugene.

"It is done."

Eugene smiled.

"Good."

49

Sadie couldn't remember the last time she felt the cold. Lying on the bonnet of the car, staring up at the stars, her mind could only just conceive of where she was.

She wanted to relax. She wanted her mind to slip into peace, to readjust to a simple, calm, translucent state. But it wouldn't. There were fires burning through her brain cells at all times, manic alertness springing from basic thought to basic thought.

Hunger burnt in her belly.

But what was the hunger for?

She didn't want to eat flesh. But she didn't want to eat vegetables, tinned food, or anything similar.

She tried verbalising this. All that came out was a grunt.

She tried to make a coherent thought, but was only able to form a few words that barely managed to represent her emotional state.

The blood surging through stung her like a wasp charging through her veins, pricking her insides as it went.

Her eyes shot open.

She sat up.

She could feel something. Sense something. Smell something.

What was it?

It was a smell that was growing closer.

She looked down the grassy verge at the wall that separated her and the sleeping child in the car from them.

It wobbled. The thick, resolute, sturdy wall wobbled. The pressure of thousands of bodies pushing against it for months forced it to buckle.

Cracks trickled along its edge. Dust brushed off the top brick as it began to slant.

Sadie jumped to her feet. Looked around herself. Gus. Where was he? Where had he gone?

For Donny.

Friend.

Donny, friend.

Now she was alone.

He told her to protect the girl.

Girl, friend.

Protect girl.

The thick brick wall slanted at an angle, shaking. The ground quivered under the strain of excessive, hungry steps.

Sadie looked back at the girl. Sleeping soundly. Not a twitch or grimace in sight. No nightmares. Just sleep.

She wished she could sleep that peacefully.

A deafening thud punched the ground. The brick wall collapsed into a dusty heap. As one part gave way, so did the rest, and at rapid pace the whole circumference of brick walls demolished amongst a heap of dust.

The undead surged forward, only to come into contact with the wire fence. They pushed against it, charging forward, pushing, desperate, pushing.

The front line of zombies were forced against the wire fence. Their faces pressed against the wiry diamonds, being pushed so hard that the wire sunk through their skin. In no time at all, the front line had lost their pale visage, turning it to pieces of square flesh falling amongst clotted blood that trickled down their chest.

The fence shook. Forced forward. Falling.

Sadie got into the car. Locked the doors. Stared with terror.

The booms against the floor provided a foreboding sense of doom. There we so many of them. So many.

Sadie closed her eyes, squinting tightly, wishing them away, denying they were there. If she shut her eyes really tightly – as in, really, really tightly – maybe they wold go. Maybe…

The earth trembled harder.

She opened her eyes.

The fence was down.

They were coming.

Sadie gently cradled Laney, ensuring not to wake her, and placed her on the floor of the passenger side. The child stirred momentarily but Sadie shushed her, and she fell back to sleep.

Sadie climbed into the space beneath the steering wheel, curling up into a little ball.

The car rocked from side to side. Nudged back and forth as body after body after body scraped past.

She watched as the zombies lurched past the car. So fast she could barely see the back of their heads. They all burst forward, fighting each other for the privilege of being first; first for freedom, first for food.

The car pounded from side to side. For a moment,

Sadie feared the car would be turned upwards, but it collapsed back to the ground and continued to shake back and forth, back and forth, back and forth.

The zombies continued to run. Continued to hunt.

She'd just have to wait this one out.

Then, amongst the ravaging horde, one zombie abruptly stopped. It paused. Waited. Hovering beside the window of the car.

Its head slowly twisted toward Sadie, whose breath caught in her throat.

It looked her in the eyes.

50

Back home. Shooting zombies on a computer game.

Donny closed his eyes and took himself back there.

It was so simple. If they got you, you'd just hit restart. There would be no difficulty in shooting them, as they were just poorly pixelated computer-generated images that were designed to explode into red pixels upon being shot. You would pick up ammo off the ground, reload, and fire.

There would be no nightmares. No difficulty in how heavy the gun was, in how to aim it. And, best of all, there would be no cannibals.

Maybe if he closed his eyes tightly enough, then opened them again, he would wake up in his room. Undisturbed and well-rested. Ready for whatever that pointless, dull day threw at him. Thinking about how desperate he was to actually do something, and being so ungrateful for the sanctity of his dark, empty basement setup.

He opened his eyes.

The moon still hung in the sky. The flickers of a fire metres away from him sent a grey smoke trickling into the air. And the happy voices of a hungry mother and daughter exchanging pleasantries sent chills through his bones.

This wasn't a nightmare. This wasn't a computer game.

He tried moving his hands. His legs. His mouth.

Everything was manically immobile. He tried wriggling away, tried squirming along the floor. He made it inches before he gave up.

Maybe the best he could hope for now was a quick death.

Would they kill him fully before they ate him? Or would they pick pieces off him bit by bit and make him watch?

What a fucked-up thought.

He shook his head at the concept of him lying there, hoping he would be given a mercy killing by two psychopathic human-eating killers.

"Fuck..." he muttered as he came to terms with the horrific nature of his predicament.

"I wish we had something to go with this," Stacey sighed.

"Oh, my darling, what would you want?"

"Some salsa verde. Or blue cheese dressing. Or hollandaise sauce, I used to love hollandaise."

"Ooh, I know. I would love to pour some peppercorn sauce over a nice bit of thigh. Oh, and do you know what my ultimate favourite was?"

"What, Mummy?"

"Béarnaise sauce. Or a bit of black bean and sesame sauce, like they used to serve at St James's in Mayfair."

"Oh, Mummy, you're making my mouth water!"

"Tell you what, my dearest – I will cook him so that it makes a bit of juice, then I will use some of that meat stock to make gravy. Would you like that? Mummy's homemade gravy?"

"Oh, Mummy, that would be delightful!"

Donny leant his head back and wept. Tears trickled down his cheeks like gentle waves. He tried to tune them out. Tried to ignore their conversation about what sauce would go best with his dead flesh.

Béarnaise sauce...

A mouthful of sick lurched up his throat and he opened his mouth to let it trickle out behind the duct tape.

"Ew, Mummy, he just vomited!"

"Oh, how revolting! What a horrible, disgusting young man!"

"Oh, Mummy, it's putting me off my food."

"Tell you what, I think it's time. Why don't you grab the knife and slit his throat?"

Stacey beamed up at her mother.

"Really, Mummy? Can I?"

Trisha bent down and lovingly pinched her daughter's cheek.

"I think you deserve it!"

Stacey grabbed the large, curved blade from her mother's belt and skipped over to Donny, her pigtails bouncing from side to side.

She bent down over Donny, a wide, innocent smile consuming her eager visage.

Donny wriggled. Tried to roll. Tried to do anything he could to get away.

"Now come on! Hold still! I can't do this if you don't hold still..."

He cried out, his moans muffled by the duct tape stuck to his lips, but he cried out anyway. Tried to scream, tried to object.

As he rolled onto his side, he saw something.

Something in the bushes.

A pair of eyes. Watching him.

Whose eyes were they?

Then he saw their lips, and a finger that moved slowly and carefully up to them, signalling that Donny needed to shush.

Donny lay still.

Stacey mounted him, her skinny, bare legs spread from beneath her frilly skirt across his chest.

She was wearing a bib. Donny hadn't seen her put it on, but she was wearing one. Around her neck.

"Oh, this?" Stacey acknowledged. "This is a really lovely dress, I don't want your blood on it."

She lifted the knife into the air.

Her grin intensified.

"Daddy showed me how to do this really well. I bet you all the pool tables in our billiard room I could do it in one clean shot."

A rustle from the bushes made her freeze.

Trisha suddenly turned around, distracted from the fire. She picked up a gun.

The bush rustled again.

Trisha fired the gun into the bush, a quick succession of bullets that she waved from left to right and back again.

Someone cried out in pain.

Donny recognised the voice.

It was Gus.

They got him.

51

A painful memory cascaded over the cinema screen of Gus's mind.

A mask around his face to block out the dust. Some voice ringing in their ear saying they had just landed in Helmand Province. Like he cared where he was – all that mattered was that their battle against the Taliban was well fought. He pushed off the helicopter to an avalanche of bullets. The helicopter sailed back up into the sky as he and his comrades sought shelter.

Then that man. Firing, repeatedly firing. Narrow eyes above a large black beard. Even though the man was firing from a distance too far to build up a recognisable image of what he looked like, he could recognise two things – that beard, and the 8-bolt-action Kalashnikov assault rifle sending bullets soaring his way. He remembered it, because he hadn't expected to see a World War II weapon being held by the Taliban – and because one of its bullet flew into his calf as he ran to the next bit of cover.

But he wasn't in Afghanistan anymore. He was in a bush, just outside London, and he was in seething pain.

It was that same calf that stung again, like a thousand wasps digging into it. He could feel the blood trickling down his ankle, but couldn't feel that ankle.

It had gone numb. For all he knew, it may not even still be there.

He cried out in pain. He tried not to. He needed to save Donny, save the girl – but he couldn't help it. He fell onto his back, sweat pouring down his forehead and flooding his eyes. He rubbed them, trying to remove the blurs from his vision, but it seemed to do nothing.

Do not pass out.

He just kept repeating those words. However bad the immensity of the agony was, however much his scar cased around the engrained bullet stung with his newly opened wound, he just kept telling himself that.

The bullet had scraped him in the worst place possible.

Do. Not. Pass. Out.

He pushed himself to his feet, clutching his weapon, putting all his weight on his one good foot. Limping out of the sanctity of the bush, he held his gun at the daughter and the mother. The mother stood by a fire and the girl held a knife over Donny, who was restrained and gagged.

"Do not move or I'll–"

He reluctantly placed a small amount of pressure on his right foot and his leg gave way. He collapsed, his face thudding into the mud below, and the gun fell out of his hands. He reached for it, but all he could think about was the pain. Shooting through his leg. Like a million zombies were digging their sharp nails into his shin.

He had to look down to check his foot was still there. His knee was agonising, but below the calf, he felt nothing. The bullet fired at him had only scraped past, cutting a chunk of his flesh off, but it was enough to reignite the anguish he had felt in Afghanistan.

"Look, Mummy," said Stacey. "He's come to save his friend!"

"Oh, isn't that sweet!"

Donny's head turned toward Gus. His eyes were wide open, tears accumulating in the, pupils full of terror. Gus knew he'd been the last potential salvation for Donny. But just as quickly as that hope had come to Donny's eyes, it faded.

He was sprawled out along the floor like a helpless baby. In too much pain to form coherent thoughts, his machine gun laying out of reach.

His calf stung like fire. It seared through him. Made him unable to focus on anything but the agony. The pure, unadulterated agony.

It went blank. But only for a second.

He felt his consciousness lose out, felt himself slipping away.

He imagined a bucket of water being thrown on his face.

He kept saying those words.

Must. Not. Pass. Out

He reached for the machine gun, but Stacey had kicked it a metre away from his hands, and out of reach.

His arm stretched. It was the only thing he could do. He was thinking in actions now. His ability to form words or thoughts had gone, gone with the burning sensation firing from his knee downwards. All he had was actions now. And the remaining action he saw was him reaching for that machine gun, taking it, and firing it into those cannibalistic bastards.

Stacey stepped on his outstretched hand. Despite it being just the weight of a young girl pressing down on his knuckles, it added to the sensations he was already experiencing and forced an ugly cry to leak from his lips.

Donny's face was beside his. Looking back at him. Hope giving way to fear.

"I'm sorry, Donny..." Gus whimpered. He hadn't thought to say it, hadn't even thought to speak, but it came out.

He blinked a few times, each time worrying that his eyes would not open again.

He reached for his machine gun.

Trisha walked forward, ripped the ammunition from over Gus's shoulder, and threw it into the distant woodland. She picked up the machine gun, emptied the bullets into the bush, then threw it at Gus's prying hands.

There was nothing left in it now.

The sweet, innocent, pretty, young girl held the sharp blade above her head.

Gus looked to Trisha. His eyes pleading to her.

He looked to her eyes, to her hands, to her gun... Her gun, over her shoulder...

Gus's eyes widened.

It couldn't be...

But it was...

He recognised the gun over her shoulder. Recognised it, as it had been used against him before.

Just as a plan started to form, he looked up into the eyes of the girl grinning down at him.

"Look, Mummy. Now we have dessert."

52

The monster's eyes were like a pair of rotten apples. Behind the yellow flare was a fiery absence, an inbuilt desire to eat, and a shuddering evil that meant it would do so at any cost.

Sadie remained frantically still.

Maybe it hadn't seen them. Maybe. And any moment now, that zombie would turn around and continue with the stampede of the other zombies on their great escape.

But no. Its salty, torn face remained, twisting as his hollow eyes clamped onto its next meal.

Its head twisted to the side. And, although a zombie did not feel emotions, she felt certain she saw the slight twitch of a smile.

The main bulk of the infected had gone. Left behind were the stragglers. This did not give Sadie any relief, as there were easily still hundreds.

The zombie turned. As if Sadie's completely stationary state had convinced it that she was nothing. That she was not worth hanging around for.

That's when Laney's eyes bolted open and she accompanied her immediate terror with a deafening, high-pitched scream. Her breathing continued to quicken pace, straining under its frantic surges of breath.

The zombie turned back, as did all the others in the vicinity, attracted to the sound of the little girl's scream. Within seconds, the car was surrounded by an audience encompassing them in a circle of rank flesh. Their hands furiously beat against the windows, their bodies ran against the car as if they didn't understand that there was a barrier in the way. Some of them thrusted their open, snapping jaws against the window, reaching for Sadie and Laney, eagerly chattering their teeth for them.

Before Sadie could take any salvation from being within the sanctity of the car, the window beside the driver's seat cracked under the force of a continual headbutt. The zombie repeatedly launched its forehead forward, like the back feet of a bucking horse. The crack grew larger until the zombie managed to smash its head through it, shattering the glass.

Laney screamed again.

Sadie quickly stuck a hand over Laney's mouth, giving a shush sign by placing her quivering finger over her lips.

The horde descended upon this open window, trying to reach inside, hands after hands after hands clambering for her.

She could fight. Hell, could she fight. But she'd fought dozens. Could she fight hundreds?

She remembered what Gus had told her.

Laney.

The girl.

She was to protect her at all costs.

With the screech of an eager predator, she leapt upwards and clamped her teeth over the arm of the nearest zombie. She clenched her teeth hard until she ripped the arm clean off, and threw the bloody remains from her mouth to the backseat.

She swung her arms forward, driving her fist into the nearest zombie and getting it stuck in its face. She wrenched her hand out of the stretched eye socket and the zombie fell against the other zombies, its visage an ugly, contorted mess.

Another zombie threw its jaw forward and clamped its teeth around her shoulder. With a sickening cry, she pushed her shoulder toward the frame of the window, squashing the zombie's skull under her strength. Its face and body fell off, leaving its jaw still clamped on her. She ripped away the teeth and continued fighting.

And in that moment, she formed a thought. The first coherent thought she'd manage to think beyond basic grunting of various motivational words.

Still alive?

Bitten.

But still alive.

How?

She let out an almighty war cry and dove out of the open window, taking the creatures to the ground.

53

"No, no!" Gus cried.

He reluctantly pushed himself to his feet, reaching his arm out for the gun over Trisha's shoulder. He couldn't think of anything beyond getting that gun. If he could just lay his hands on it, just take it for a moment, then maybe…

"Aw, look at him," Trisha teased. "He's trying to get my gun."

"What a featherbrain!"

Stacey smiled at her mother and they shared a loving hug.

"Now, we have a choice to make. Originally, we were going to eat the scrawny one – but this one has far, far more meat on. What do you say?"

Gus groaned, reaching out for the gun, opening and closing his fist as he helplessly grasped.

"Do you really, really want this gun?" Trisha asked, a face full of bemusement. "Here, have it!"

She took off the gun, fired it into the bush, emptying it of all bullets, and chucked it on the floor just out of Gus's grasp.

He didn't wait a moment. He reached his hands for it, digging them into the soil, dragging himself forward, ignoring the pain, just dragging himself closer.

If he could just get his hands on it...

"I just emptied the clip!" Trisha laughed loud and heartily. "This one is such a simpleton! Look at him! Reaching for a gun that's completely empty!"

A glance back at Donny's face.

Eyes still wide. Tears still trickling. Face full of terror.

The pain in his calf was still seething, but he had become accustomed to it now. If he pretended it didn't exist, he still felt it, but it helped him to keep going. To stay conscious. To reach for that gun.

He dragged himself closer. It was nearly within reach.

"Are you not listening to me?" Trisha taunted, a mocking, patronising smile etched across her face as she bent down to him like you would a dog trying to get a snack. "There are no bullets in it. You won't be shooting us with that."

He dragged himself closer.

Ignored her. She can go to hell. She can go fuck herself.

He reached his hand out, landing it on the gun, grabbing it tightly.

"I think we should wait to kill this one. I'm worried he may be on drugs, and I don't want us getting them in our system," Trisha continued. "I mean, honestly, my darling, have you ever seen something so peculiar?"

"It is most bizarre, Mummy. Honestly, it's like I'm watching one of those comedy sketches again. What were they called, Mummy? The ones Daddy used to watch with me?"

"Laurel and Hardy, my darling, Laurel and Hardy."

"Yes. It's like them. Absolutely hilarious."

Fuck. You.

He turned on his back, holding the gun across his chest, holding it tightly against himself.

"Saying that, those gunshots may have attracted some nasties. We really should be getting on with it."

"Okay, Mummy."

Stacey walked toward Gus.

It didn't matter.

He held the gun.

The gun, that just so happened to be an 8-bolt-action Kalashnikov assault rifle.

And he had a bullet for it lodged in his calf.

Minus Zero Minutes

Rick Wood

54

Sadie's arms thrashed and smashed, her feet kicked and soared, and her jaw snapped down on the throats of her victims.

That's how she saw them. Victims.

The undead.

Those that were bitten.

Like her.

She threw another zombie over her shoulder, kicked the loose leg off another, sending it to the ground, then plunged her fist into the gaping throat of another.

But they kept coming.

No matter how many she turned to pieces of helpless flesh and grotesque guts, there was always another to take its place.

But she had to get through them.

She had to protect the girl.

She couldn't let Gus down.

A grey arm with muscle tissue falling out of a gaping hole managed to get past Sadie and to the car door, reaching in for Laney. Sadie ripped the arm off and stuffed it down the throat of the opposing zombie, then launched her fist into its guts, pulled them out, and sprayed its entrails over the floor below. The helpless zombie slipped on its own guts and struggled like a dying fish.

She killed another. Then another, and another, and another.

Eye gauges. Ripping out throats. Plunging their heads into the ground and stomping them to pieces.

The ground surrounding Sadie turned into a graveyard of decaying insides.

But more still came.

Then they all stopped. Hovered motionless for a fleeting moment.

Without any warning or reason, each paused.

Then, as if sensing an imminent distinct danger, they sprinted away. The remaining few running, putting distance between themselves and danger. What was it they heard? What had they sensed? What could they smell?

Then Sadie understood, as she smelt it too. Her basic instinct took over and told her to run, the same instinct that ruled those fleeing zombies. A distant oncoming odour of smoke, so sensitive to her nose that she wasn't even sure she smelt it.

Then the sound came. The rumble growing louder, the thudding of propellers in the air, the soaring of aerodynamic resistance bringing with it immense danger.

She looked to the sky.

There it soared, a plane, shooting overhead. As it travelled into the distance, something from it dropped. A large whirlwind of fire raised into the air. The bomb in the distance, beginning the attack on London.

She felt the ground tremble, shuddering beneath her. It was in the distance, but the tremors still sent her falling onto the ground. The car lifted upwards, then landed back down to earth.

That was one bomb in the distance. Enough to take away her balance and raise a vehicle from the ground.

How had the infected known? For all of them to just suddenly start running, in unison, away from the bomb?

Then she remembered what Gus had said about the Taliban.

The guns and the fists and the knives, they all did some damage to 'em – but it was the bombs and grenades that really showed us who they were. Cowardly instincts of an animal told 'em to run. They knew then.

The sound resumed. More engines, more speed, soaring overhead.

She looked upwards.

A plane flew overhead.

Then another.

Then another.

Until so many filled the sky, she couldn't register the quantity that was approaching.

And she knew the instinct of the infected was to run, because hers was the same, just amplified. And as she watched the planes slow down over London, her instinct changed from a tremble to a manic roar.

55

Stacey loomed over him. The picturesque ideal daughter, the model image of clear skin and a beaming smile. Pigtails. Frilly dress. Loving, doting eyes toward her parents.

Gus plunged his fingers into his gaping wound.

He wailed and moaned and cried and screamed. It hurt like hell, but the bullet that had skimmed past him had created enough of an open wound that he could reach his hands right in and pry the scar tissue apart.

It felt rubbery. Fat spilled out over his fingers, like he was pushing into a juicy steak. He could see a pool of blood filling the floor, but he tried not to look at it.

He just had to stay conscious. Ignore the pain.

He screamed harder. It hurt too much.

He paused. Breathing. Taking a break.

But the knife held high above the girl's head told him he had no such opportunity.

It was inches away.

She was taking her aim.

Thoughts escaped him. He relied on instinct. Pure, basic instinct.

He pushed his fingers further in, opening his leg until he felt it. That small, metal cylinder, lodged between a bone and muscle. Stuck in there.

He ripped it out, screaming from the excruciating anguish, watching as blood sprayed like a streak of piss over the soil.

"Whatever are you doing?" asked the girl, ready to strike.

No time to think.

No time to suffer.

Just got to do it. Put the bullet in and do it.

He opened the pistol grip of the Kalashnikov, slotted the bullet in, and pointed the gun at Stacey's cute little face.

"Where on earth did you get that bullet from?" she asked, the knife poised above her head as her confused expression gazed down at her food.

BAM!

Her face exploded into a hundred pieces. The bullet soared through her, sending splatting pieces of brain, skin, and a wayward eyeball soaring in every direction.

"Stacey!"

Trisha sprinted over in despair. She dove upon the headless body of her daughter slumped heavily upon the blood-soaked earth.

Gus didn't waste any time.

He stole the knife from the girl's hand and dug it into Trisha's calf.

She wailed out in pain.

He grimaced. It was a nasty place to get wounded. He'd know.

As she fell to her back he retracted the knife and put all his energy into lifting himself up. Raising the knife above his head he pushed it through the air, and sent it plunging downwards into her throat.

Her choking and splattering didn't last long. The

blood continued to squirt over Gus's already drenched clothes until her face fell lifeless, as did her empty body.

They needed to hurry. She would turn soon.

He turned to Donny.

There were four of him. Four heads, all spinning around in circles.

Blurs turned to inky splodges. His vision faded to hazy shapes.

His head spun like he was drunk, turning around and around, despite him being desperately static.

"Donny…"

He reached out for his friend, then fell to the floor and passed out.

56

It took Donny every strength in his body, everything he had, to pull Gus. Donny had hold of Gus's one good leg as he pulled the hefty, unconscious weight across the dirty earth, leaving an imprint of his body in the mud as he did.

He'd already seen the planes firing overhead. He'd felt the tremble of the ground upon the impact of one bomb.

Now there were how many planes?

At least thirty. Maybe even forty.

Too many flying too fast for him to count.

Adrenaline grew tired in his veins. He'd been running on it for so long now that he felt the onset of his comedown, just as he needed it most.

But still he gripped, tightening his fingers around Gus's thick ankle, dragging him.

Donny could just leave him.

But he knew he wouldn't.

Gus saved him whilst running on empty, it was time to do the same.

The tremors of another bomb twisted his legs into submission and he fell onto the ground. His face smacked harshly into the mud.

But he got up.

Brushed it off.

Persevered. Gus would never fail his mission, now it was time that he didn't fail his.

He pulled again. His muscles wouldn't do it. They were aching too much.

He paused. Let his breath catch up. Let his body regather itself.

"Come on," he urged himself. "Come on!"

He tried to pull Gus, but it was dead weight that wouldn't budge.

He fell to his knees.

"No…"

He couldn't do it. He couldn't drag him, he didn't have the strength; he didn't have the willpower. He was going to have to leave him. He had no choice. Otherwise he'd die too.

He had no choice.

He lifted his eyes to the sky. Harsh droplets of water began to pound upon his face. Slowly at first, then faster. Faster and faster. Until they were parading helplessly into his eyes, drenching his clothes, soaking his hair.

The last of the planes disappeared overhead.

He had minutes, if that.

"I'm sorry, Gus."

He turned to Gus, who groaned in his unconscious state and allowed his hand to flop onto his jacket. There was something beneath Gus's hand. Something in his pocket.

Donny reached inside the jacket. Wrapped his fingers around whatever it was and pulled it out.

In his hand was a pair of sunglasses.

He cradled them like a baby, gazing upon the cool

shades, completely torn between running and staying.

Those sunglasses. Gus had brought them back for him.

To shut him up.

No. It wasn't just to shut him up.

It was to show him who he could really be.

He placed the sunglasses on, wearing them proudly. He was an action hero. He was a secret agent. He was Bruce Fucking Willis kicking the bad guy's arse in *Die Hard*.

Those zombie computer games don't got shit on a badass like me!

And he would not leave his friend behind.

With a desperate scream he grabbed Gus's ankle and lurched it forward. And again. And again. And again.

He screamed with the agony of his muscles.

But fuck it.

Gus had wrenched a bullet from his body for him, Donny could damn well endure the pain within his muscles it took to drag this big lump.

"Argh!"

He dragged. Dragged. Dragged.

"Son of a bitch! Bastard! Motherfucker!"

The cursing helped ease the pain.

Before he knew it, he came to an opening.

Sadie stood beside the car door.

"Open it, Sadie! Open the car door!"

She did.

"Help me put him in."

Sadie took Gus's head and Donny took his good leg. It took them a few attempts to lift him fully, but they managed to throw him in a quick surge of energy, dumping him onto the backseat.

Donny passed his jacket to Sadie.

"Wrap this around his wound, stop the bleeding."

Donny rushed to the front seat.

Another few bombs pounded the streets of London and the car jumped a foot into the air from the tremors that sunk along the ground.

The flickers of flames and the grasping hands of the smoke reached out for them.

Donny did the quickest three-point turn he had ever done and turned the car around. He slammed his foot upon the accelerator.

Another few bombs sent the earth shuddering, and the car almost capsized. Donny twisted the steering wheel in an attempt to keep it straight, and just about managed.

In the windscreen mirror, he saw London go up in flames. The tremble of the earth continued onto the motorway. And, although it grew fainter the further away they got, he could still see the fire rising into the air for miles.

Once they were far enough away, Donny looked over his shoulder at Sadie, who had managed to wrap both his jacket and another blanket she'd found somewhere in the car around Gus's leg, and it looked like less blood was seeping out.

Gus's eyes flickered open momentarily.

"What…" he muttered.

"Relax, Gus, relax," Donny urged him.

Gus looked to Donny. His weak eyes showed a vague recognition.

He held out his hand, and very faintly said one final word.

"Friend…"
Then his head dropped, and he passed out.

Rick Wood

Plus Fourteen Days

Rick Wood

57

The faint pulsating beeps of hospital equipment stirred Gus from his sub-conscious. His eyelids fluttered. His vision faded from a hazy blur to sharply defined lines as he dazedly twisted his neck from side to side.

Light beamed between the blinds of the window. As he looked down, he took in the sight of a faded hospital gown. His eyes trickled down his body until they reached his leg.

He'd already been fitted with a prosthetic foot.

He leant his head back, closed his eyes and exhaled. He should have expected it, really.

"It was quite the effort, Mr Harvey," came a well-spoken yet aggravated voice.

Gus twisted his head to the side, casting his eyes upon the disgruntled face of the prime minister. Eugene sat with his arms folded, a face coated in loathing.

"How's... your daughter?" Gus managed, finding his voice croaky from lack of use.

"My daughter? She died six months ago."

"Have I been out that long?"

"No, you have been out for two weeks. That girl you saved was not my daughter, you imbecile."

Gus grew confused. Before he had time to answer,

Eugene had left, with those words left to linger.

If she hadn't been his daughter – then who on earth had he rescued?

The days went by, and Gus heard little more. The doctors came to pass him small portions of indigestible food three times a day, but they said little to him.

He asked them questions every time.

"Where's Donny?"

"Is Sadie all right?"

"Where's the girl?"

After a few weeks, he gave up asking.

He wondered about Donny. Why he hadn't come to see him.

He could remember little about what had happened after he'd killed the cannibal family, but he could remember glimpses. One definite glimpse that remained in his thoughts was Donny's face, looking down at him.

"Relax," Donny was telling him.

And Sadie. She was alive. She'd spoken to him.

Where was she?

He tried to get up and leave his bed, tried to walk upon his prosthetic, but the first twitch of his arm sent an alarm ringing and doctors flooded the room. He didn't hear the words they shouted, but once the commotion had ended, he had been restrained to the bed. His arms and thighs were fixed into position with straps. From then on, he was fed through intravenous drips.

*

One morning, Gus awoke to a chilling cold. His breath appeared before him, like the cool smoke of a cigarette, and he felt his skin prickle with goose pimples.

"Hey! Hey, I'm cold in here!"

He didn't know why he bothered, no one listened.

His head turned over and looked at the single window in the room, which was covered in frost – both on the inside and out.

As he turned his head back, a recognisable figure appeared in the doorway.

"You…"

Eugene stood still. His arms were folded, his face bemused.

Gus frowned at him.

"So you keeping me prisoner here now?" Gus asked.

Eugene didn't reply. He slowly shook his head, licked his lips, then nodded at someone outside the room. On his command, three soldiers entered the room. One of them stuck a needle in Gus's thigh, and he felt his limbs go limp.

"What is this?"

The answer presented itself without the need for verbal confirmation. It was a paralysis agent, to stop him from thrashing against them. He felt his muscles fall limp and knew that struggling would be futile.

The soldiers unstrapped Gus and placed him on a wheelchair. They wheeled him down the corridor, following Eugene, who walked at some pace. Then ended up in a lift.

Gus glared at Eugene for the entire descent. Eugene did not return his look. Instead, Eugene kept an unmistakable visage of loathing, like something had perturbed him greatly and he was infuriated about it.

Gus finally realised why he was there. Eugene needed to know something he knew. And, if Gus was there, Eugene had no other line of enquiry to follow.

They reached the bottom floor, which was poorly lit and smelt of damp. They took him to a room with a one-way mirror. Behind it was darkness. The soldiers halted his wheelchair against the wall in the small room lit only by a flickering bulb.

Eugene leant against the wall and waited. Bided his time before nodding to the soldiers.

The soldiers vacated, and it was only Eugene and Gus left in the room.

Eugene allowed silence to prevail. He appeared in no rush to speak, but the disdain wiped across his face remained clear and unbreakable.

"Who's the girl?" Eugene finally mused, slowly and calmly. If Gus hadn't figured out the circumstances of the interrogation, he would have said that Eugene's tone was casual – but Gus knew that he was the one in control. If he had information to impart, then he was being kept alive for that reason, and to be forthcoming would be foolish, no matter what they did to him.

"What girl?"

Eugene gave a bitter snigger, each jolt of laughter conveying sarcasm and irritation.

"Who. Is. The. Girl," Eugene repeated.

"You'll have to be a little more specific. I've known a lot of girls in my time."

"I'm going to ask you one more time, and I promise you, if you do not give me an answer, you will live to regret it."

"Will I?" Gus retorted, his lip curling into a smirk.

"The girl you found, and you returned with. Says her name is Sadie, amongst little else. Covered in bite marks, yet she lives, not as one of the infected, but as one of us. Who is she?"

"Sadie? Sadie…" Gus stuck his bottom lip out. "No, doesn't ring any bells."

Eugene shook his head.

"Okay then," he muttered, "you want to play it that way."

Eugene beat his hand against the one-way mirror twice, and the scene on the other side of it instantly lit up.

The room was full of men in white coats, with clipboards, in various discussions, surrounding something. As they parted to reveal what that something was, Gus's mouth fell open and his world fell apart.

Sadie. Stood horizontally off the ground, restrained to a board. Fasted by her waist, wrists, and ankles. Unclothed, wearing nothing but a dozen bite marks.

She couldn't move. She wriggled and fought against it, but it did nothing. She was trapped, but she didn't seem to be able to understand any more about why she was there than an ant would understand why a child was trying to stomp on it.

She squealed and screeched, wailed and moaned, roared as hard as she could, but she was not able to communicate her distress, nor could she understand its reasoning.

"Let her go."

"Who is she?"

"Let her go!"

With Gus's further reluctance to answer, Eugene beat his hand against the window twice more.

A man in a white coat pressed a button, and Sadie's wails filled the room. She shook with the seizure of a high voltage of electricity soaring through her body.

"Perhaps you could let us know when you are more forthcoming," Eugene spoke. He left the room and the soldiers returned, taking him away.

Gus watched Sadie disappear as he was wheeled out of the room, but the echoes of her pain could be heard all the way down the corridor.

Within minutes he had been returned to his room and restrained once more to his bed.

He was left alone.

With nothing but his thoughts.

All alone.

The hours ticked by. As did the days.

The doctors left him. There was no food. No help. He was left to completely to his solitude. With nothing.

But Sadie's face remained. The torturous look on her face.

On the face of the girl who had taught him to love again.

The whole time, two thoughts punched through his mind. Two questions, stirring around the forefront of his mind, bubbling with the heat of boiled anger.

How he was going to rescue her.

And how he was going to beat the life out of Eugene Squire until there was nothing left but the remains of an undead corpse.

Chronicles of the Infected

Book Two coming in 2018

Join Rick Wood's *Reader's Group* to stay up-to-date with upcoming releases...

and get more of Rick's books for free!

Join at
www.rickwoodwriter.com/sign-up

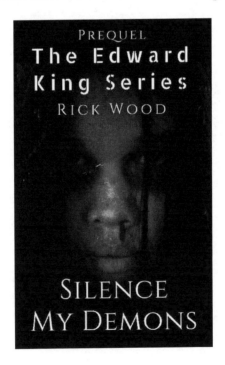

Also available from Rick Wood

The Sensitives

Made in the USA
Lexington, KY
19 June 2018